I0673901

SHELTON IN LOVE

Dianne Hartsock

A NineStar Press Publication

www.ninestarpress.com

Shelton in Love

© 2021 Dianne Hartsock

Cover Art © 2021 Natasha Snow

This is a work of fiction. Names, characters, places, and incidents are either the product of the author's imagination or are used fictitiously. Any resemblance to actual persons living or dead, business establishments, events, or locales is entirely coincidental.

All rights reserved. No part of this publication may be reproduced in any material form, whether by printing, photocopying, scanning or otherwise without the written permission of the publisher. To request permission and all other inquiries, contact NineStar Press at the physical or web addresses above or at Contact@ninestarpress.com.

Printed in the USA

ISBN: 978-1-64890-308-3

First Edition, June, 2021

Also available in eBook, ISBN: 978-1-64890-307-6

WARNING:

This book contains sexually explicit content, which may only be suitable for mature readers.

SHELTON IN LOVE

Chapter One

Shelton ignored the flutter in his stomach he always experienced when invited into Nevil's room and settled back into the cushions of the chair. "Who's the lucky color?" he asked, trying to feign indifference.

Nevil drew a pair of socks from the top drawer of the bureau at random. "Ah, the gray ones."

"What? Percy again? Didn't you have him earlier in the week?"

"So what? These socks have never let me down," Nevil countered and rubbed the soft wool against his cheek, purring like a happy kitten.

Shelton's stomach knotted at the decadent smile on Nevil's face. Nevil had made it clear when they had first met he'd enjoy sleeping with him. The jealousy eating Shelton now was his own fault, but was it wrong of him to want more from Nevil than a passing fling?

He shoved away the thought of sharing a meaningful relationship with Nevil, knowing it could never happen. However, the desire made Nevil's flirtation all the more hurtful. "Fine, but if you make the man fall in love with you, you can buy us an answering machine and listen to his calls when I'm not home. I don't want to hear him whine when you break it off."

Nevil looked at him, raising a finely arched brow. "Who says I'll break it off?"

"Get real. You'll be bored in less than a week. Remember Daniel Pratte? You scarcely managed six days with him after swearing to all who'd listen you'd love him forever. He called for weeks after you told him it was over, hoping you'd be the one to pick up the phone. Admittedly, he was a bit of a prig, but I'm the one who had to listen to him sobbing his heart out. I refuse to do that with Percy."

"Danny wasn't the right man for me. I haven't made up my mind about Percy." Nevil unknowingly twisted the knife deeper into Shelton's heart. Shelton held his breath when Nevil sat back against the headboard and lifted his foot onto the bed, pushing up the cuff of his tan Dockers. Moistening his lips, Shelton fought his attraction as he watched Nevil pull the sock over his foot and up a muscular calf. He was a faithful jogger and in May already had the beginnings of a fabulous tan.

Shelton's treacherous gaze followed the fine dark hair up Nevil's leg until it disappeared under the cuff of his pants. Captivated, his gaze continued upward to where the fabric tented nicely at the juncture of his thighs. His heart skipped a beat when Nevil shifted on the bed and the material pressed against a definite bulge.

Panicked, he raised his head, hoping Nevil hadn't observed his interest. Nevil's beautiful blue-green eyes watched him; then Nevil cocked an eyebrow. Shelton pushed to his feet from the chair, his face burning at Nevil's slightly mocking smile. "I'm going to make a sandwich. Do you want one?"

"No, thanks. I need to save room for dessert," Nevil reminded him as his tongue flicked over his lips. An image of Percy's nicely rounded butt in tight jeans flashed through Shelton's mind.

"Suit yourself," Shelton muttered, watching as Nevil crossed his legs to leisurely pull on the second sock. Tearing his gaze from the provocative sight before acting on the impulse to join Nevil on the bed and strip him of clothing, Shelton left the room and stomped to the kitchen, grabbing meat and cheese from the refrigerator. He swore under his breath as he slathered mayonnaise on the bread, hating Percy and every other man represented in the myriad of colored socks in Nevil's top drawer.

Eating at the counter, he glanced up to find Nevil leaning against the door frame watching him. Shelton wondered what the thoughtful look on his face meant.

"Do you have plans?" Nevil asked after a moment.

"Tera wants to do a photo shoot down by the lake."

"Now? The sun will be down in an hour."

Shelton shrugged. "She's your sister. Think you can talk your twin out of a course of action when she's made up her mind to do it? I can't."

Nevil snorted. "Neither can I." He straightened. "Well, I'm off. See you later, darling," he said as if they were a couple. Shelton felt the blood mount in his cheeks, infuriated by his callousness. Nevil had to be aware of his feelings for him. Why did he feel it was necessary to flaunt his lovers in his face?

Remembering the sandwich in his hands, he glowered at it, no longer hungry. Climbing off the stool, he tossed the sandwich in the garbage under the sink, wrinkling his nose at the ripe odor that wafted from the canister.

Shelton's shoulders slumped, and he leaned a hip against the counter, discouraged. Maybe it was time to admit defeat and move out. He and Nevil had become friends when his firm had hired Nevil's architectural company to design their new office building. They'd moved in together when the project was completed, Shelton finding Nevil's dark good looks, dry humor, and moments of gentleness on the edge of irresistible.

He'd hoped that with proximity, the attraction between them would grow into a more lasting connection. He let out a dejected breath, realizing it was his own fault it hadn't. Shelton had never shared with Nevil the true reason why he wouldn't sleep with him.

I'm afraid. It's that simple.

The few relationships he'd had in the past had ended badly, leaving him embarrassed and heartbroken. Despite how much he longed to try again with Nevil, the thought of being vulnerable again terrified him. He didn't think he could survive Nevil's rejection.

Thoroughly out of sorts with himself, he pulled a jacket from the closet and left the apartment to meet Tera at the park. It was a short walk, and to his surprise, he rather enjoyed the crisp air with its hint of summer to come in the warm breeze. The wind ruffled his brown curls, and he smiled to himself, knowing Tera loved that windswept look in her photos.

Humor restored, he trotted along the path through the trees to the picturesque lake at the park's center. He spotted Tera setting up the mobile spotlight between two maple trees close to the shore and waved when she glanced at him, ignoring the thud of his heart. She was a softer, feminine version of Nevil with her luxurious dark hair in a chignon at her neck.

Shelton swore under his breath, not wanting to think about her brother and what he was probably doing with Percy at that moment.

Eyes the same incredible blue-green as Nevil's flashed at him as he came up to her, and she rose on her toes to kiss his cheek. "Hello, dear. Hurry, the light's perfect." Tera made an urgent motion toward the portable dressing room.

Shelton chuckled, already stripping out of jacket and shirt as he crossed to the curtained booth. Tera was always in a rush, bursting with more energy than two or three other people combined.

Stepping into the booth, he changed from jeans into the coffee-brown slacks and white dress shirt hanging on the rack. Slipping his arms through the ivory-colored vest, he slung the coffee-and-tan tie around his neck and returned to Tera's side, tucking in the shirt as he went.

Shelton glanced up at a low whistle, feeling the tingle of a blush starting under Nevil's appraising eyes. He tried to stifle a surge of excitement that Nevil had come to watch the photo shoot when he hadn't seemed interested earlier. Plans must have changed with Percy.

"You dress up nicely," Nevil assured him as he stepped closer and batted Shelton's fumbling hands away from the tie. "Let me do that."

Shelton concentrated on Nevil's fingers on his tie, urging his heart to stop racing before Nevil felt it pounding under his fingertips. Nevil's breath brushed his cheek, and his spicy cologne sent his senses whirling.

Why was he so damned attractive?

Shelton hardly noticed Tera slipping his arms into a jacket until Nevil commented on it, rubbing the silk and wool material between his fingers. "Nice."

Shelton glanced at his sleeve and admired the sharkskin pattern of taupe, tan, and black checkers. He shrugged his shoulders, delighted with the fit and comfort of the sport coat. "A new one?" he asked Tera.

"I've had the design finished for months but couldn't decide if it should go in my summer or fall catalog."

Nevil finished with the tie and stepped back, looking Shelton up and down. "Definitely summer, though I'd wear a coat like that all year round. Almost any color of slacks would go with it."

"Or socks," Shelton muttered a reminder to himself as Nevil ran his fingers through his hair, sending sparks of desire through his body as he mussed his curls.

Nevil tilted his head to take in the overall effect. A lazy smile spread on his face while a warm gleam entered his fantastic eyes. "Delicious." His gaze lingered on Shelton's shoulders before sliding down to his hips.

Shelton wished he'd buttoned the coat as he felt a twitch in his groin, his body perking up at the attention. The whirl of the camera in Tera's hand recalled him from the tantalizing thought of Nevil's hands on him as well as his gaze, and Shelton moved to stand under the soft light she'd set up to complement the glow from the setting sun.

He thought he'd feel awkward with Nevil watching while he posed, but instead found Nevil's presence exhilarating. Shelton knew he looked his best, and Nevil's admiring attention bolstered his confidence. Ignoring the stares of a few passersby, he flirted with the camera, losing his inhibition as Tera called encouragements and clicked frame after frame, only calling a halt when the sunlight had gone.

"These are lovely. They'll fill out the catalog nicely," she commented, tilting the camera to show the men a few of her favorites.

Nevil whistled at one in particular where Shelton had glanced at the camera through lowered lids, a secret smile playing on his lips. The overhead light brought out the highlights in his chestnut hair and lightened his hazel eyes, complementing the warm colors of his ensemble for an overall attractiveness.

"You'll need to stockpile this coat, Tera," Nevil observed, his eyes never leaving Shelton's. "Every man who sees that picture is going to want one for his own." His gaze was intense, and Shelton colored at the innuendo.

"I'd better change."

Nevil grabbed his tie as he took a step away, stopping him, his smile widening at Shelton's exasperated breath. "Can we borrow the suit, Tera? I want to take Shelton out for a drink in it. The boys will love it."

Shelton made a halfhearted protest, and Tera came to his rescue. "Maybe he's tired, Nevil."

"Then a drink is just what he needs, especially after working in that stuffy bank all day."

"I'd say he needs his sleep. Being the financial advisor to a bunch of corporate bigwigs can't be easy."

Nevil planted his fists on his hips. "Neither is designing condos for a bunch of snotty businessmen. Yet I'm going out."

Shelton listened as they discussed him, part of him longing to go with Nevil, though the thought of spending an evening with Nevil thrilled and terrified him at the same time. It would be hard to keep his resolution not to sleep with Nevil after a few drinks, especially when Nevil already stole his breath with a smile. He wondered with an uneasy detachment what they would decide to do with him.

He wrinkled his brow at a depressing thought. "What happened to Mr. Gray Socks?" he asked, unable to keep the derision from his voice. Damn, he hated this feeling of jealousy, but he couldn't seem to help it.

"He had to work late. God, Shelton, it's only a drink. I'm not asking you to strip for me." He put a hand on his shoulder, and a hot flush of desire swept through Shelton at the touch. Erotic images of the two of them together flashed in his mind, and Shelton had trouble focusing on the rest of Nevil's comment. "Come with me. You'll have fun and I'd love to hear you laugh tonight."

Shelton glanced at Tera, who nodded. "I can pick the suit up tomorrow."

"No, you don't," Nevil put in, bowing slightly. "I'll personally have it dry-cleaned and delivered to you."

Tera laughed and pushed Nevil toward his Prius parked at the curb. "Idiot. Go on." She patted Shelton's cheek as he hesitated. "Enjoy yourself. It's okay to have a little fun."

Shelton watched her bite her lip, her gaze lowering like it did when she was worried.

"But..."

"You know how my brother is. I love him to pieces, but he and you…"

Shelton sighed as she stumbled over her words. "He'd never date someone like me."

"I've never known him to seriously date anyone, and you're too nice. Don't let him hurt you."

"I'll be careful," he promised, but she was still frowning.

"Robert's gone for the weekend on a business trip." She hesitated, concerned but plainly not wanting to interfere. "If things get too crazy at home, come stay with me for a bit."

"I'll be fine," he assured her, but she didn't smile as he thanked her for the loan of the suit and hurried after Nevil.

Chapter Two

To Shelton's surprise, Nevil took him to one of the more subdued pubs in Portland, saying he didn't want competition for Shelton's attention. Shelton sighed in relief as he slipped into the booth and settled against the comfortable leather cushions. He'd been half afraid Nevil would take him to one of the boisterous clubs he frequented. This was a more intimate setting, but there were enough people milling around for him to keep his head with Nevil.

A tingle of excitement filled Shelton when the waiter took their order, the man's eyes showing interest as they flicked over him, further bolstering his confidence. Nevil laughed softly, but it sounded warm rather than mocking, filling his heart.

Nevil leaned toward him across the table after the waiter brought their drinks. "I'm glad you're here. Everyone's jealous of me."

Shelton snorted, but his heart lifted at the praise. Curious as to why Nevil had said that, he sneaked a look around the crowded room and startled at a man openly staring at him. Caught, the blond picked up his drink from the bar and walked toward them, never taking his green eyes off Shelton.

Sliding into the booth beside Nevil, the man gave Nevil a familiar kiss on the cheek. "Who's this, darling? Lovely jacket."

Shelton felt instantly self-conscious. "Thanks. It's a Tera Shaw."

The man snapped his fingers. "That's where I know you! You're right, Nevil, the man's as gorgeous in real life as he is in the catalogs."

Shelton stared at his drink, heat burning his face under the stranger's steamy gaze. When had Nevil discussed him with this man? Shelton didn't even know the guy. What had they said?

Nevil picked up his glass and swirled the contents, his eyes focused on the reflection of light in the amber liquid. "Now you've seen him. Shouldn't you be getting home to the boyfriend, or are you going to solicit an autograph?"

The man made an irritated sound, but then his expression changed as he looked from him to Shelton. "Oh, I get it. Want some privacy." He gave Nevil a broad wink. Tossing back his drink, he then slid to his feet. "Well, gotta run. You two have fun." He gave them a leer before pushing his way through the group of people clustered around the bar.

Nevil scowled at his retreating back, then turned a rueful face to Shelton. "Michael Barns is an ass even at work. Ignore him. I try to."

They both glanced up as they heard their names being called, and Nevil left the booth to embrace the couple approaching them. "Steve and the lovely Sara." He kissed Steve's pretty wife on her cheek. "Join us."

"Hi." Shelton shook hands with Steve as the couple sat across from him, relieved to see friendly faces. Sara raised a questioning brow when Nevil slipped onto the bench beside Shelton. Shelton gave her a smile in return, his blood racing as Nevil's thigh brushed against his own. Sara was a coworker and one of the few friends who knew of his feelings for Nevil. Shelton wanted to share his hopes with her but kept silent, having no idea where the evening would lead.

Nevil pushed tighter against him as several more of their mutual friends joined them at the booth, sending up a cheerful call for drinks. Intensely conscious of his growing erection at Nevil's closeness, Shelton swallowed his drink down when it came. The liquid left a pleasant muddle in his head, stilling his panic as the heat from Nevil's body sent his pulse hammering.

At one point, Nevil leaned against his shoulder and loosened his tie, running his fingers up his neck to muss his hair. "Told you this would be fun," he teased and gave him a light kiss on the lips.

What did he mean?

Nevil swiveled back to their friends as if nothing extraordinary had happened, but it had shaken Shelton to his patent leather shoes. God, he wished Nevil would take him home to his bed.

Shelton sobered at the thought, his heart plummeting as he recalled the socks in Nevil's top drawer.

So many colors.

He couldn't compete with that. Wasn't sure he even wanted to.

Nevil glanced at him and leaned closer to whisper, "What's the matter? I thought we were having fun."

Shelton swallowed the lump in his throat, feeling like a fool. "We are. I'm sorry, I guess I'm tired."

A frown crossed Nevil's face, but then he looked thoughtful. His mischievous smile tugged at the corner of his lips. "I'll take you home, love," he murmured, before raising his voice. "Excuse me, everyone. Shelton wants me to take him home."

Amid the general laughter and the movement of bodies, Nevil slid off the end of the seat and held out his hand to Shelton, a challenge in his blue eyes.

Ignoring the proffered limb, Shelton said good night to the others and struggled to his feet, the last drink having sent a pleasant tingle along his nerves. Nevil gave him a dazzling smile as he swayed a little, and the tremor turned to fire, igniting Shelton's blood. Nevil's gaze became smoldering, and he put a hand on Shelton's elbow, guiding him from the pub to his car.

Shelton slid into the passenger seat while Nevil held the door, watching him as he settled in. Then with a swift move, Nevil bent down and kissed him full on the mouth, sending shocks of electricity straight through Shelton.

Nevil lingered over the kiss, bringing a startled moan from Shelton as pleasure churned in the pit of his stomach, slipping down to his more intimate region. He couldn't get enough of Nevil's taste, nor the way his tongue twined with his own, seeming to wrap around his soul.

He was bereft when Nevil left him to circle the car to the driver's seat. Without a word, Nevil slipped the key in the ignition and started the engine. Shelton became acutely aware that his hand rested only inches from Nevil's thigh as he shifted gears, grinding a few in his hurry. They exchanged a grin, and Shelton's pulse thundered in his ears. Terror gripped him, but he pushed it down. He had to trust someone again, sometime.

Shelton's heart constricted at the thought. Frantic, he closed his mind to the possibility of rejection, wanting this night with Nevil, aching to have the gorgeous man in his arms, pushing into him. It would be worth any heartache that followed.

Nevil parked the car in front of their apartment and shut off the motor. His beautiful eyes blazed as he gazed at Shelton, and Shelton could hardly breathe when Nevil touched his cheek. Nevil shifted in his seat and leaned over to claim Shelton's mouth again with his own.

The kiss was different this time, urgent, masterful, drawing an instant response from Shelton's love-starved body. Nevil's tongue plundered the soft lining of his mouth, sliding in and out until Shelton's head was spinning with a nameless yearning. He slipped his own tongue between Nevil's lips and thrilled at his soft moan. The scent of Nevil's cologne became a pleasure in itself: alluring, bewitching him, swamping his doubts in an overwhelming need.

Nevil's kisses burned down his neck and Shelton leaned his head back to give him access as he deftly undid the buttons on his vest and the shirt beneath, spreading them open to expose his chest. Shelton's tie was still in place, in stark contrast with his white skin. Stifling a decadent laugh in his throat, Nevil rubbed the silk over one of his nipples, sending a tingle of pleasure through him. Nevil nipped the opposite bud, and this time the current jolted straight to Shelton's groin, making him cry out in surprise. He was instantly aroused, his dick straining against the confining clothing holding him in.

Nevil's lips teased at the hardened bud on his chest, then returned to his mouth for another shattering kiss. "We should have done this ages ago," Nevil murmured appreciatively, slipping an arm around Shelton's waist to lift him closer.

A horn blared, and headlights swept through the windows, a car pulling out of the parking lot with a squeal of tires. Nevil loosened his hold, chuckling as he drew away from Shelton. "No one's done that to me since high school."

Shelton stayed where he was, panting and slightly dazed. Nevil took his hand, kissing his fingertips. His eyes lingered on Shelton's heaving chest. "I could take you right here," he confessed, his voice unsteady. "But let's go inside. I need a little more privacy for what I have in mind."

Shelton flushed, heat coursing through his whole body.

Pulling his clothes together, he fumbled for the door handle, chilled as he stepped outside the car. Nevil came around the hood and took his hand, pulling him toward the apartment door.

Nevil hardly waited until the door closed behind them before capturing Shelton's lips in a hungry kiss, flipping on a light before urging him back toward the couch against the wall. Once there, he stopped and eased the coat from Shelton's shoulders, placing it over the back of a chair.

"Can't have Tera angry with us," Shelton observed, though he didn't care at the moment.

"No indeed," Nevil teased and promptly pushed him onto the couch. He put his hands on Shelton's shoulders and gave him a lingering, drugging kiss that turned Shelton into jelly. Nevil's pliant lips traveled his jawline and down his neck, planting little kisses on their way to his chest.

Nevil nudged Shelton's knees apart and knelt between them, his fingertips burning along Shelton's sides to play with the button of his slacks while he licked at Shelton's nipples. Shelton whimpered as the plucked nerves sent jolts of pleasure through his body to his balls and onto the tip of his growing dick. He ached to have Nevil's lips there, sucking him.

Nevil deftly unfastened his pants and panic crashed through Shelton. "Don't," he whispered, his stomach knotting as all his fears sprang into his head. He couldn't go through with it after all. He hadn't explained anything. He felt nauseated, his mind screaming as Nevil continued to pull at the zipper. "Please, don't."

Chapter Three

Nevil's eyes flashed up in surprise at his tone, and Shelton covered his face, pain choking off his breath. Better to be lonely than risk Nevil's revulsion, though it hurt more than he had thought possible. Nevil gripped his wrist, but Shelton wouldn't show his face. "What is it?" Nevil demanded.

His concern touched Shelton's sore heart, but he could only shake his head, helpless to explain.

"I know you want me," Nevil said, puzzled. He stroked Shelton's hard cock through his black briefs to prove it, making him shudder with need and leaving a longing for more. "Is there someone else?"

Shelton found it impossible to answer him. Easier to let him have a peek. After jerking his head no, he leaned back on the cushions and tightly closed his eyes, granting Nevil permission to do as he liked.

Nevil gave a bewildered mutter and nudged Shelton's butt off the couch so he could remove his briefs. Shelton heard Nevil's sharp indrawn breath as he bit back an oath. The silence tortured him, and he fumbled to cover himself.

Nevil grabbed his wrists. "You were circumcised?"

Shelton nodded once.

"The butcher," Nevil bit out, fury underlining his words. "A doctor did this?"

"When I was a baby. He was sued for malpractice soon afterwards for another incident and lost his license, but it was too late...for me." He choked out the last words, wanting Nevil to know it wasn't his fault.

"Do the scars hurt?"

Shelton made a soundless cry of pain at the question. He struggled when Nevil's arms went around him, scalding tears filling his eyes. Nevil kissed his eyes and cheeks and lips, murmuring endearments until he calmed.

Nevil tipped his chin, making Shelton look him in the eyes. "Someone's hurt you because of this?" he asked, his tone demanding an answer.

Shelton gnawed on his lips. He'd never told anyone about the agony he'd endured countless times.

"My lovers never stay," he said, misery underlining his words. Humiliation returned full force. "The last one laughed at me. He said I should sell tickets. People would pay to see—"

Nevil stopped his words with a hard kiss. His lips softened into a caress. "Forget that bastard," he murmured in his ear. "When I asked if it hurt, I meant does it hurt you physically when you make love."

Hot blood rushed to Shelton's face, but he knew Nevil wouldn't let the question go. "It's been so long, I don't remember," he lied and pushed at Nevil, all at once overwhelmingly tired. "Let me up."

Nevil pinned his shoulders to the couch with his strong hands. "No," he said. He shifted, and Shelton gasped in shock as he took his cock, scars and all, into his mouth.

God! He'd never felt so... The sensation was...

Shelton couldn't catch his breath from the waves of pleasure flooding his body, scalp and hands prickling as the pressure built deep inside him, straining toward his erection. Shelton's balls tightened as if all the pain and shame and loneliness of life gathered there. Unable to stop the orgasm, in one giant surge of ecstasy and anguish he came in Nevil's mouth, emptying out until only a pleasurable delight remained as Nevil continued to suckle on his softening dick.

Reality struck Shelton, and he groaned, throwing an arm over his eyes. He sank into the couch, wanting to melt away. He imagined the hours Nevil must spend with his lovers, and here he'd come after just a few licks of Nevil's tongue. He was a freak. God, he wanted to *just not be there* anymore.

With a last kiss on his tip, Nevil pulled Shelton's briefs back up around his hips. Shelton heard his sigh and wouldn't blame him if he left. He jumped a little when Nevil nudged his arm aside and cupped his cheek and brushed a tear off with his thumb.

"My poor boy, don't be embarrassed." Nevil placed a soft kiss on his lips and stood up when Shelton remained silent. "You've had a hard evening. Come to bed."

Shelton didn't resist when Nevil helped him to his feet. When they reached the hallway, he started for his room, but Nevil steered him determinedly toward his own bedroom and Shelton was too tired to argue. Once there,

Nevil urged him under the covers, kissing his cheek as he burrowed into the pillows.

"Sleep, love," he whispered gently. "We'll talk in the morning."

Shelton didn't reply and heard Nevil sigh again. He lay still as Nevil rooted in his dresser for something; then he picked up his car keys.

"I'll be back soon," Nevil said vaguely and stepped into the hallway. In a moment, Shelton heard the apartment door close and wrapped his arms around his chest, his heart aching as he wondered what color of socks Nevil had taken with him.

He slept in fits and starts, listening for Nevil's return. After a rather unpleasant dream of being lost in a parking garage, unable to find his car, he awoke and squinted in the soft light from the lamp on the bedside table. Nevil rummaged in his top drawer again. Catching his eye, Nevil gave the drawer a shove closed, looking dismayed, as if he hadn't wanted Shelton to see him in the bureau.

"Good, you're awake," he said and climbed on the bed with Shelton. Nevil kissed him, sliding his hand down his chest and under the blankets to caress him through his briefs. Shelton's dick hardened at his sure touch, his heart pounding from Nevil's appreciative murmur as he continued to rub him through the soft cloth, sending currents of bliss through Shelton's body.

Nevil pulled his polo shirt over his head, exposing his nicely toned chest dusted with dark hair. His tan glowed honey gold in the lamplight, and Shelton raked an appreciative gaze downwards to where the dark curls disappeared into his Dockers.

Nevil undid the fly and inched his pants off his slim hips, exquisitely slow, building Shelton's desire until he feared he'd combust with the heat licking at his nerves. With a sudden tug Nevil was free, his erect cock and tight balls spilling into the light, perfectly molded, more beautiful than Shelton ever imagined.

Nevil laughed at his stare, his lips curling into a smile, and leaned over to kiss him. Shelton caught his wrist as Nevil reached for the dark briefs still hugging Shelton's body.

"We can turn the light off," he offered, wanting to spare Nevil another glimpse.

"Like hell." Nevil deftly slipped the encumbering garment off Shelton's hips, down his legs, and tossed them across the room. To his chagrin, Nevil then gathered Shelton in his arms and proceeded to give him soft kisses. His touch was achingly gentle as he stroked his back and arms, his fingers feather-soft on his skin.

Shelton wanted to scream, needing so much more. Made desperate by Nevil's careful touch, he rolled and pinned Nevil under him, cursing in his frustration. "I won't break, goddammit!"

Nevil grinned at him. "There you are, love. I wondered what it would take to rouse that delicious passion I see in your eyes when you're angry."

"I'll show you passion," Shelton murmured before smashing his lips on Nevil's, drowning in his delicious taste. God, he wanted this. Nevil moved sinuously under him, his delight in Shelton's body obvious. Nevil drew his knee up between Shelton's legs, and Shelton groaned as it pressed into his cock and balls. The friction as he rubbed his dick against Nevil sent torrents of pleasure through him that caused sparks behind his eyes.

Shelton remembered to breathe and met Nevil's twinkling eyes. "Don't pass out on me," Nevil teased, nuzzling his throat. "We've hardly begun."

Stretching his body in delight, Shelton gave himself over to Nevil's skillful lips, tongue, and fingers. He was brought again and again to the brink of release, only to have Nevil ease off until he could think straight again.

In one moment of blissful delirium, he took Nevil's gorgeous dick in his mouth, experimenting with his tongue over the rigid shaft, nibbling and licking the dripping tip. He'd forgotten it could be so mind-blowing to suck on another man's arousal. Nevil's shout of pleasure as Shelton kissed and suckled one of Nevil's balls drove him to the brink.

Nevil sat up, pushing him away. "You have to stop, or I'll lose it right now," he panted, squeezing his shaft at the base.

"Would that be so bad?"

"No. Maybe..." Nevil rubbed a hand over his sweating forehead. "God, Shelton, you have me so dizzy I can't think. Maybe you should get inside me now."

Emotion overwhelmed Shelton, aroused and trying not to make a fool of himself by blurting out how he really felt about Nevil. How he loved him.

Seeing his panic, Nevil kissed him, fondness warming his eyes. "Just lie on your back and let me take care of you."

Shelton settled on the sheets and stared at the pool of light on the ceiling, his chest heaving. He never knew

Nevil could be so kind. His desire for Nevil poured from Shelton's heart and flooded his body. He trembled, knowing he would soon be inside Nevil and closer than he'd been to anyone in his life, though he'd had sex before.

Nevil leaned across the bed, digging around in the side-table drawer, and then straddled his legs. Shelton had never felt so exposed, the ugly head of his erection standing between them. He gasped in disbelief, thrilling as Nevil purposely kissed the glistening tip with its irregular patches of dark skin and ragged scar tissue.

With a final lick, Nevil sat up and squeezed lube onto his fingers, giving Shelton a lurid wink as he reached back and wiggled a finger into his ass. Shelton moaned with him, heat and lust rushing through him as Nevil stretched himself open. Nevil parted his lips in a soft gasp, and Shelton had never seen anything more lovely than Nevil's face flushed with pleasure. Nevil bent down and brushed his lips over Shelton's. "Want to help me?"

"God, yes."

A smile spread across Nevil's face, and he tossed Shelton the bottle of lubricant with his free hand. Shelton fumbled with the cap, spilling more on his chest than he got on his fingers. Nevil's warm chuckle thrummed along his sensitized nerves and Shelton held his gaze while he ran his fingers down Nevil's back and lower, traveling the crack of his ass. Nevil's lids fluttered and closed, a choked cry escaping him when Shelton's hand found his and Shelton slid a finger into him. God! Shelton couldn't wait to have that tight heat gripping his dick.

Nevil wriggled as the fingers worked inside him with small sounds of pleasure escaping him. "Another one," he gasped, and Shelton widened his eyes. Nevil laughed, sounding breathless. "You're larger than three fingers," he assured Shelton. Shelton snorted, though he was absurdly pleased with the avowal.

It proved a tight fit to squeeze another finger into Nevil's body, his dick growing painfully hard as he imagined all that warmth surrounding him. Unable to help himself, he ran a finger of his free hand up Nevil's cock, gathered the drop of precome on the head, and brought it to his mouth. Nevil's taste burst on his tongue and he groaned.

Nevil pulled off his fingers, resting his sweaty forehead against Shelton's. "Enough. Need you inside me," he murmured and kissed him. He moved down Shelton's body to sit on his thighs again. Opening a foiled package, he proceeded to roll the condom down Shelton's hard dick, driving him wild as he massaged his balls before adding the lubricant. "Ready?" he asked as he positioned his butt to take Shelton in. Without giving him a chance to answer, he pushed down.

So tight! But then he slid past the initial resistance and could thrust up into Nevil. His triumphant cry rang with Nevil's shout of quick discomfort and absolute bliss. When Nevil regained his breath, he rocked forward, pulling himself to the tip of Shelton's cock, then plunging down again, beginning a rhythm that drove Shelton senseless with pleasure.

"God, Nevil. I don't... I can't...stop..." He gasped, unable to halt the climax building inside him.

"Then don't," Nevil said as he reached back to squeeze his balls, sending an incredible jolt of pleasure bordering pain through him. Shelton's body tingled, a buzz starting in his head as all his energy focused downward, rushing to gather for that final ecstatic thrust.

Reaching blindly, Shelton caught Nevil's cock in his hand, stroking him while he thrust into Nevil's hot depths. His head was reeling at the twin sensations of power and rapture far beyond thought. Shelton let him go to grab Nevil's hips with both hands, pushing wildly, frantically, the pressure building until it released in a shattering orgasm into Nevil, Shelton breathing Nevil's name, lost in joy.

He returned to himself by slow degrees, becoming aware of Nevil lying on his chest, grinning.

"I think you enjoyed that," Nevil teased, then eased off of Shelton and settled his length beside him, stretching his lean body. "So did I."

Shelton gazed at him, then lowered his hand and felt stickiness between them. "I wanted you inside me," he said, not bothering to hide his disappointment as he reached for a tissue on the bedside table for the condom.

Nevil laughed out loud. "Glutton. It's your fault I came. Don't worry, I'll get my turn. But right now, we've got to get some sleep. Morning's coming all too soon and we both have to work."

"Damn. You're right."

Nevil chuckled as he turned off the light and snuggled down beside him.

Chapter Four

Shelton roused, sluggish, pulling a pillow over his head at the familiar sound of the shower being used. Then he came fully awake. Damn. What time was it? After a glance at the clock, he scrambled from the covers and trotted down the hallway to the guest bathroom. Turning the faucets, he stepped under the hot spray of the shower and soaped his body, rubbing at sore muscles he hadn't felt in ages.

As he rinsed the suds, he looked at himself for the first time in a long while and sighed. The ragged scars where the doctor had unevenly cut the foreskin, then cut again to try to correct his inept work, stood out clearly. But it did look as if the silicone gel he'd been applying had somewhat faded the dark patches and smoothed the scar tissue. And he remembered with some smugness that, even though Nevil was beautiful, Shelton was the thicker of the two. That had to count for something.

Thoughts of their incredible night together sent Shelton hurrying from the shower and back to Nevil's room, ostensibly to retrieve his abused briefs, but in reality, he wanted to catch a glimpse of Nevil's delicious body before he dressed and maybe steal a kiss or too.

He paused in the open doorway. Nevil was already dressed and sitting on the edge of the bed, slipping a pair of light blue socks on his feet.

"Pretty," Shelton said before he thought.

"Your favorite color, I think?" Nevil asked, lifting a socked foot.

"Yes," Shelton managed to say, though it felt as if Nevil had squeezed his heart with his hands. So that was where Nevil had gone last night, to buy socks to represent him. He wondered helplessly how often he'd be chosen from among the others already in the top drawer.

Feeling dazed, he spotted his boxers against the far wall and crossed in front of Nevil to retrieve them. Nevil stood and touched his wrist as he passed, stopping him, and Shelton trembled as Nevil's hand slid up his back.

"See you tonight," Nevil said, giving him a light kiss before leaving the room. Seconds later Shelton heard the front door close.

He stared at the floor, unable to think beyond the hurt in his chest. He didn't want to see all the men he'd have to share Nevil with. But his treacherous eyes had him looking anyway, and he winced at the blue socks mixed with the other colors in the drawer. He laughed at his own absurdity. Of course he'd been a passing amusement like the others.

The clock in Nevil's room sounded loud in the silent apartment, and Shelton returned to his room to dress, hurrying from the complex to catch the light rail train to work. One of the perks of living in Portland; he didn't need to own a car.

Once there, he did try, but the day passed in an endless stream of discontented clients and meticulous, tiresome paperwork. Lunch consisted of a sandwich and coffee at his desk—he didn't care what he ate—and he left early, claiming a headache. In reality, he was unable to get thoughts of Nevil out of his head. He had the dangerous wish to be with him again. Perhaps they'd have a repeat of last night. Nevil had given Percy a week of his time. It wasn't crazy to hope for a few consecutive days, was it?

He got off the light rail a block from his apartment complex with the desire to walk through the park. The afternoon sun warmed the spring air, and he removed his coat and loosened the inevitable tie, wishing he'd gone home to change first as several joggers passed him on the pathway. He'd like to run and clear his head. He found an empty bench by the lake and sat down, smiling at the pretty scene of crocuses and tulips blooming along the shoreline.

A familiar laugh made him look up, his heart pounding as he turned his head. Nevil leaned against a tree talking in animated tones to a man who stood over him, his hand on the trunk of the tree beside his head. It was Percy, damn him, looking amazing in tan slacks.

Nevil laughed at whatever Percy had said, and Percy straightened, clearly furious with him. He grabbed the front of Nevil's shirt and pulled him close, giving him a hard kiss.

Surprised, Shelton looked around, but there was no one else to see their blatant display of affection. He was hardly aware of the pain that squeezed his chest as he dropped his gaze to his hands clasped on his lap. Nerves burning, he pleaded with the universe to be invisible so

Nevil wouldn't see him sitting on the bench. He wished the ground would swallow him up, anything, afraid to move and draw their attention.

In a moment he heard their voices drift off and he risked a glance, seeing them disappear into the trees in the opposite direction from him. He waited a few minutes, then, sick with disappointment, rose and walked the short distance home.

The apartment had an empty silence to it he'd never noticed before, and he closed the door behind him with reluctance and locked himself into the quiet, lonely rooms.

"Damn," he said, not sure what he meant by the word. Without bothering to change, he went to the kitchen, grabbed a can of soup out of the cupboard, and heated the brownish blob over the stove instead of the microwave, not minding the extra time it took. What else did he have to do, anyway? Nevil had said he'd see him that night, but he never should have gotten his hopes up.

Unthinking, Shelton took his hot bowl of soup to the living room and bit off an oath at the sight of the couch. Body instantly on fire and aching for Nevil's touch, he placed the soup on the coffee table and sat down, sinking into the cushions. Trembling, he surrendered to the memory of Nevil's skillful fingers; his talented lips and tongue bringing fulfillment. Shelton could never tell Nevil, but that night had been the best in his life.

Drawing a ragged breath, he sat up and clicked on the television before letting one mindless show after the other numb his senses and nudge him toward sleep. At one in the morning, he finally dragged his aching body to bed only to sleep in snatches, listening for Nevil to come home. It was another two hours before he heard the key at the front door and Nevil's familiar tread in the hallway.

Shelton's pulses leapt to life as Nevil's footfalls paused outside his door. He clutched the blankets, urging Nevil to come in and kiss away his hurt and loneliness. He didn't even care where he'd been. After a brief moment, the footsteps receded and Nevil's door closed firmly. Shelton rolled to his side and stared at the wall for a long while.

Chapter Five

Shelton never knew how he got through the rest of the week. After a few brief, awkward encounters with Nevil in the kitchen, it finally dawned on him Nevil was trying his best to avoid him. When Saturday arrived, Shelton woke early and hurried to the kitchen, intent on having it out with Nevil. He stared at the fresh pot of coffee in disbelief. Nevil had already been up and gone, leaving the coffee on for him.

Dropping onto a stool at the counter, he covered his face. Everything was ruined. By giving Nevil what they'd both wanted, Shelton had lost the man he loved. He laughed without humor in the silent apartment. Saturday had always been their day to laze around the table with coffee and the paper, maybe going to brunch somewhere when they woke up early enough. Apparently, he didn't even have Nevil's friendship anymore. He moaned, blinking back scalding tears at the bitter truth: no one ever stayed with him after making love.

Shelton sat up and took a deep breath, easing the tightness in his chest. Nevil had left the morning paper spread on the table, and Shelton pulled it to him, turning to the rental pages. He refused to stay with Nevil and be ignored. Shutting his mind to how swift Nevil would be to find another roommate, he read over the list of available places.

After making a list of likely rooms to rent, he changed into track clothes and left the apartment, jogging to the park to take the path around the lake. Shelton thought of when he'd seen Nevil there with Percy and increased his pace to outdistance the painful images.

He ran until his lungs burned, and then he flung himself onto a bench, his chest heaving as he caught his breath, body trembling.

"Shelton?"

He jumped with fright on hearing Nevil's voice in his ear. Nevil's face was inches from his own. With only a slight move, Shelton could reach the luscious, inviting mouth, but he resisted the temptation.

Nevil straightened and Shelton gazed up at him, defenseless, noting how beautiful he looked in shorts with his tank top clinging to his chest. Nevil's black hair clung to his forehead, damp, a trickle of sweat running alongside one gorgeous turquoise eye. Every nerve in Shelton's body strained toward him, wanting that strong, vibrant body against his own and that delicious mouth and tongue fencing with his.

He stood abruptly and pushed past Nevil without a word, ignoring his call as he walked away. It was too much. He couldn't do this and pretend nothing was wrong between them. His body ached for Nevil. He missed their friendship. Nevil had been kind when they'd made love where others had been cruel. It hurt more than he thought possible that it meant nothing to Nevil.

Shelton walked for what seemed hours, circling the lake several times before he stopped and stared unseeing at the water near his feet.

"It's better to have loved and lost..." he murmured, and a bitter laugh escaped him. Obviously, the person who'd written that hadn't gone through the hell of rejection. No, it wasn't even rejection. Nevil would delight in sleeping with him as long as there were no strings attached. It was absurd of him to ache for a lover and partner to go through life with.

A shudder traveled his body, and he nodded, knowing he would hurt for a long while, but it was time to get his list and find a new apartment. Start again. Anguish bit him, but Shelton shoved it away and set his feet determinedly toward home.

Once he reached his doorstep, he hesitated with his hand on the doorknob, not sure what he would do if Nevil was inside. It didn't matter. He'd be polite, take a shower, and catch the train downtown. With any luck, he'd be in a new apartment by the first of next week. He despaired at the thought.

Shelton knew Nevil was home the moment he stepped through the door. The scent of his spicy cologne floated on the air, the tingle of electricity in the rooms.

"Nevil?" he called cautiously.

A groan answered from the living room, and he crossed the small foyer to find Nevil sprawled on the couch, an arm thrown across his eyes.

"What's wrong?" he asked from the doorway, reminding himself severely it wasn't his problem.

"My stomach hurts, and there's a tightness in my chest," Nevil mumbled, forlorn. "I think I'm having a heart attack."

Shelton suppressed an exasperated breath. He'd learned in just a few weeks of Nevil's company that he was prone to anxiety, one manifestation being he often thought he was falling victim to one terrible illness or another. He liked it when Shelton fussed over him or perused symptom charts with him on the computer until reassured.

Going to the couch, Shelton knelt beside him, knowing if he didn't talk him through it, Nevil would worry until he fell sick. "It can't be a heart attack. Where do you hurt, exactly?"

Nevil groped for Shelton's hand and pressed it to his chest. "It hurts here."

Shelton licked his lips as heat from the toned body under his hand seeped up his arm and spread through him.

He knew the texture of the skin beneath the thin shirt Nevil wore and the salty yet somehow sweet taste of it. He wanted to put his mouth on the hardening nipple close to his fingertips and tease it with the tip of his tongue and teeth until he brought a groan of pleasure from Nevil. He cleared his throat. "When did it start hurting?"

"Monday night—no, Tuesday morning."

Shelton pulled his hand back, stung. "Not a damned bit funny, Nevil."

Nevil looked at him with a flash in his incredible eyes, and Shelton scrambled backward as Nevil reached for him. Nevil slipped off the couch, and Shelton flung up an arm, pushing against his chest to hold him off. "Leave me alone."

Nevil sat back, an impish smile on his lips. "We both know you don't mean that."

Shelton dropped his arm, the fight going out of him. "What does it matter?" he asked, staring at the floor. "You can't give me what I want. Let me go while I can still leave you. It would be kinder."

"What if I don't want you to go?"

Shelton blinked as tears stung his eyes. "Nevil, please. You know I want more than a week, or month, or half a year. It's forever with me. I'm sorry. I can't play at this."

Nevil's silence tore at his heart, and Shelton stood, keeping his face averted. Nevil rose instantly, standing close, and the heat from his body encircled Shelton in a warm, erotic blanket. "Stay with me," he said, his breath caressing Shelton's cheek.

"I can't."

Nevil closed the short distance between them until their bodies touched. His lips nuzzled Shelton's neck. "But I want forever."

Shelton pulled his head back to look at Nevi's face, feeling battered with pain. "Why would you hurt me like this? We were friends... I thought so, anyway."

"Shelton, love, what do you think? I'm old enough, and certainly have been around enough, to know what I want. It's you, darling. I've fought against it all week, but when you walked away from me at the park today, I was afraid it might be for the last time. When you didn't come home afterwards, I was terrified that I might be too late. That I'd already lost you."

He picked up Shelton's hands, kissing them. "Say I'm not too late."

Shelton had never heard Nevil plead before. "But are you sure—"

Nevil silenced him with a hard kiss. "I was quite happy being a bachelor until I found myself thinking of you at the end of the day. I wondered what you were doing—who you were with. Damn, who'd ever think someone like me could fall so much in love? But you're charming, and witty, and beautiful..."

Shelton's face clouded. "Not all of me is beautiful."

"Ha!" Nevil shouted, startling him, and a warm flush spread through his body as Nevil leaned closer to whisper, a smoldering look in his eyes, "Your cock's deliciously rough, Shelton. What man could resist you pushing into them, driving them mad with pleasure?"

Nevil's hand dropped, kneading Shelton through his clothing. He turned his head, and Shelton followed his gaze to a trash bag full of colored socks. "Only blue socks for me from now on."

"Damned right," Shelton murmured, distracted as Nevil's thumb stroked his growing erection, sending spirals of electric bliss through him. He wasn't a fool. He knew Nevil had said this about other men. About Percy. But maybe Nevil would give him the chance to prove he was the one to make him happy. Shelton wanted that chance.

Surrendering, willing to risk his heart to the man he loved, he pushed him backward until Nevil ran up against the couch.

"Sit down," he said on a ragged breath. Nevil promptly sat, his eyes widening with surprised heat, probably at Shelton's demanding tone. Shelton knelt between his knees and pulled Nevil's shirt over his head. His hands shook as he slipped off Nevil's jogging shorts, leaving the dark briefs on for now. Bending down, he lifted Nevil's foot and rubbed his cheek against the soft fabric of Nevil's sock. *His* sock.

Desire flashed through him at the sight of the golden skin emerging from the soft blue material. After planting a kiss on the muscular calf in his hands, he licked and stroked his way up to the lighter skin of Nevil's inner thigh, delighting when Nevil's breath quickened. His lips hovered over the tiny, provocative button on Nevil's boxers, looking up when Nevil put a finger under his chin, raising his face.

"I love you, Shelton," Nevil said earnestly and leaned to cover Shelton's mouth with his own before Shelton could reply. They kissed urgently, thoroughly, Shelton's heart overflowing with love and joy at Nevil's declaration.

"I love you too. Always," he promised as their lips parted. Shelton caressed Nevil's jubilant face with his hands and lips. Fully aroused, Shelton dropped his gaze back to the tiny button on Nevil's briefs. Quickly unfastening it, he swirled his tongue against the heated, delicious decadence of Nevil's hard cock and balls, catching fire when Nevil groaned and arched his back off the cushions begging for more. Shelton was more than happy to oblige.

SHELTON'S

PROMISE

Chapter One

"Damn," Shelton swore as he stepped from the commuter train into a bitter wind. Putting up the collar of his coat, he hurried along the sidewalk, hoping to beat the storm home. The first snowflakes stung his face before he reached the brownstone apartment he and Nevil had recently moved into. He smiled with relief when he spotted Nevil's Prius in the driveway. Good. He wouldn't have to worry about Nevil driving in the bad weather.

As he inserted his key into the front door lock, Shelton's mood lifted further with the thought of being home. It had been a long week, and he looked forward to relaxing on the couch with a beer and the hockey game on TV. Nevil would grumble about it, sitting at his feet and picking the game apart. Bored, he would fixate on one of the more handsome athletes, talking dirty until at last, he'd crawl over Shelton's body and take out his kindled imagination on his obliging lover.

Shelton patted his coat pocket, reassured the small jewelry box he'd picked up that morning hadn't been misplaced. After six months with Nevil, he wanted to take their relationship one step further. Excitement ran through him as he imagined Nevil's amorous response to his gift. Feeling more than a little aroused, Shelton eagerly pushed open the front door.

Synthpop dance music pounded from the bedroom stereo as Shelton closed the door on the storm. He removed his shoes in the foyer and set them neatly beside Nevil's before making his way down the hall. Pausing in the bedroom doorway, he leaned on the frame. By the loud music and clothes strewn on the bed, Nevil dressed to go out in his usual, untidy way. Shelton chewed his lip, remembering the snow.

Nevil glanced up from the buttons on his dress shirt, and an attractive smile slid across his face. Shelton felt his bones melt under Nevil's admiring gaze. "Good. You're here. Hurry up. We're going to be late as it is."

Shelton's spirits fell. "What are we doing?"

"Stewart's birthday?"

"God, is that tonight? It's snowing outside."

Nevil walked over and helped him out of his coat. "Don't be silly, love. We get snow here every year." He pushed the tie to one side and then unbuttoned Shelton's shirt. "Oh my." He spread his hands over Shelton's chest. Licking Shelton's lips, he lingered over a kiss, brushing his thumbs across Shelton's nipples, sending pricks of electricity along his nerves.

Nevil drew back with obvious reluctance and pushed Shelton toward the bathroom. "You have ten minutes."

"You could join me..." Shelton invited, but Nevil grinned and shook his head, waving him off. Shelton stripped out of his work clothes and then headed across the room to the bathroom. Once there, he turned on the faucets of the shower and stepped in, moaning as the hot spray hit the stiff muscles between his shoulder blades. Shelton soaped up and enjoyed a moment of guilty pleasure as he slid his hand over a growing erection, roused by Nevil's attention. He would have loved to continue and bring himself to orgasm, but Nevil slammed a drawer in the bedroom, reminding him of the time.

Rinsing off, still fondling his balls, Shelton wondered if Nevil would help him with his problem. He glanced down at his dick and sighed, wishing they were staying home.

When the last of the suds had slipped down the drain, Shelton turned off the water and opened the shower door, startled to find Nevil holding a towel. A smile spread over Nevil's face, and Shelton shivered in anticipation at the gleam in the lovely blue-green eyes.

"I guess we'll be even later than expected," Nevil purred. He walked up to Shelton and leisurely dried his body with the towel. Nevil took Shelton's erect cock in the soft cloth and rubbed it between his hands, and Shelton whimpered with mindless pleasure.

Nevil knelt on the bath rug, and Shelton had trouble catching his breath when Nevil sucked on the tip of his aching dick. He blinked at the tears stinging his eyes, his chest swelling with love as Nevil kissed every ugly patch of skin and scar tissue. How had he ever lived without this sweet lover? Sparks went off behind his eyes when Nevil engulfed him as if wanting to swallow him whole. Nevil's tongue left him breathless.

As the familiar, glorious pressure built, Shelton touched the back of Nevil's head, urging him to slow down. Nevil snorted and palmed Shelton's shaft, stroking him as Shelton slid in and out of Nevil's hungry lips.

Driven wild by the opposite sensations of Nevil's rough hand and the wet suction of his mouth, Shelton came with embarrassing quickness. Threading his hands in Nevil's hair, his mind reeled as Nevil swallowed his seed.

"Oh God," he said raggedly, watching as Nevil continued to suckle him even though he'd softened. Nevil slowly moved his head back and kissed the tip as Shelton slid out of his mouth. Shelton dropped to his knees, still panting, his body tingling with pleasure. Nevil's face was flushed with passion, and Shelton leaned forward to kiss the last traces of spunk from Nevil's lips, the flavor of it subtly different from Nevil's own delicious orgasm. He kissed his way up to Nevil's ear. "I want you inside me when you come," he said, knowing it was Nevil's favorite thing to do.

"Later," Nevil whispered back, touching Shelton's face and giving him a loving kiss. "I want to think about you during the party."

Heat flushed Shelton's face at how easily Nevil could arouse him. "What if I don't want to wait?" he countered, starting to unbutton Nevil's shirt.

Nevil batted his hands away. "Too bad," he teased and rose effortlessly to his feet, leaving Shelton kneeling naked on the floor. Nevil smiled down at him, his gaze fond, running a hand through Shelton's chestnut curls. He tilted Shelton's chin up and kissed him one more time. "Get dressed, love. I'll warm the car."

"Are you sure that's what you want?" Shelton made a grab for him, but Nevil skipped out of reach. Shelton heard him laughing as he left the room. When the front door slammed, he dressed in haste but took a moment to transfer the jewelry box from his suit to his winter coat pocket and turn off the stereo. Shelton crammed a tan snowcap over his hair and pulled on his gloves as he left the house. The snow had begun to stick, and he walked gingerly over the ice slicking the pavement. He could see his breath in the cold air and wrapped his scarf tighter against the chilled wind but was shivering by the time he reached the car.

Climbing into the passenger seat, he noted that Nevil wore his black leather coat and cap. Nevil looked darkly handsome, his blue-green eyes startlingly beautiful as Nevil glanced at him. He smiled with affection, and Shelton's heart swelled.

"Can't we stay home?" he tried one last time, not eager to be out in the storm. And he wanted to give Nevil his gift in private that night. He'd been thinking about it all day.

"Don't be stupid," Nevil said cheerfully, steering the car into the street. The car slid a little on the dusting of snow, and Nevil slowed down to a safer speed, though he teased Shelton about his white knuckles on the dashboard. It took twenty minutes to cross town, and then they were climbing into the hills, Nevil slowing further as evening shadows settled in and the snow thickened.

Usually, it was a beautiful drive into the woods, but as the car slid more often on the curves, Shelton gritted his teeth, wishing they'd stayed home like he wanted. He didn't breathe freely until they parked in the line of cars in Stewart's driveway. Nevil left the Prius with a look of anticipation on his face, but Shelton walked at a slower pace through the slush before climbing onto the porch a few steps behind Nevil.

Stewart answered the door, and they shared an animated greeting, Nevil disappearing with Stewart into the crowd. Shelton took a minute to talk to Stewart's wife, though he shuddered as she drunkenly flung her arms around him. "Shelton, darling!"

"Andrea." He nodded, removing her hands with force from his butt and stepping around her into the house. He shrugged out of his coat before shoving it into her hands to stop her from unbuttoning his shirt as well. "Thanks for inviting us," he called over his shoulder, winding a path around couples on his way to the kitchen. He caught Nevil's laughing eyes on him from across the room and scowled, realizing Nevil had left him with the woman on purpose. Really, Andrea's aggressive advances were enough to make any man's pride perk up. Didn't mean he liked it, though.

He found safety in the kitchen where he grabbed a beer. He headed for the den, hoping someone was watching the game. Sure enough, the second period of the hockey match had already begun, ice flying on the TV screen. Ignoring the couple making out on the far end of a couch, Shelton nodded to the few people he knew in the room and settled into the cushions to watch.

He took a swallow of the cold beer. *God, I'm tired.* He never should have come out with Nevil. He didn't have the energy for one of Stewart's parties. His eyes grew heavy, and a dream formed behind his lids of a warm bed and soft pillows and Nevil's arms before someone leaning over the couch startled him awake, their hands running over his chest.

Nevil chuckled in his ear. "Did I wake you? Come out with me. I'm lonesome." He tugged on Shelton's sleeve.

Shelton obediently followed Nevil to the door, still trying to shake the sleep from his head when Nevil stopped him, guiding him to a dark corner of the room. Nevil backed him to the wall and pressed against him.

"I could eat you alive," Nevil murmured over his mouth, then started a long, drugging kiss. Nevil sucked on Shelton's tongue, drawing a response from his dick.

Shelton cupped the back of Nevil's head and held him in place as he returned the kiss, exploring Nevil's luscious mouth. He wondered vaguely what man at the party had ignited Nevil, but then didn't care when Nevil caressed his chest and slid his hands to the bulge growing in Shelton's pants.

"Do you want to go home?" Shelton asked with hope when Nevil let him breathe, remembering the gift in his coat pocket. He wanted to give it to Nevil now and drown in Nevil's exuberant response.

"We just got here. Come on. I want to show you off." Nevil slipped an arm around Shelton's waist and urged him toward the kitchen. Conscious of the weight in his trousers, Shelton felt his face tingle with embarrassment when they joined the group at the bar. Someone shoved a drink into his hands, making him happy. If Nevil was going to torture him all night, at least Shelton didn't have to take it sober.

Nevil kept Shelton close as they pushed through the crowd in the living room to reach the couches. Shelton's heart dropped to his feet as they joined the group and he spied Percy sitting in an armchair, looking splendid in jeans and a close-fitting blue sweater.

Percy raised his brows on seeing them. "Look, our lovely Shelton is here. How are you, dear?" he asked, his tone dripping sarcasm. Shelton wanted to smash the smirk off Percy's face as gray eyes looked him over and dismissed him. A smile of satisfaction touched Percy's full lips. "Is he protection, Nevil?"

"I don't know what you mean, darling," Nevil said coolly and pulled Shelton to a spot on the couch as another couple left. Shelton made small talk with the people around them, all the while catching glimpses of Percy's gaze locked on him. Nevil leaned back on the couch, driving Shelton to distraction by playing with his curls. He pulled one of them, and Shelton met his gaze, his breath catching at the fire smoldering in the blue-green depths.

Nevil unexpectedly reached for the empty glass Shelton had been rolling in his hands. "Here, let me get you another drink."

Shelton murmured a protest, but Nevil had disappeared into the crowd. Turning back to the girl he'd been talking with, Shelton encountered Percy's intent stare and gasped, stunned. No one had hated him so openly before. Jealousy and pain glinted in his wide, gray eyes, and Shelton shivered slightly.

Percy sat on the edge of his chair. "You need to get out from behind that desk and into the sun, darling." He tilted his blond head. "Or are you coming down with the flu? You're quite dull this evening."

Shelton studied his nails. Percy was currently drowning his sorrows in a college freshman, and Shelton couldn't help getting in a dig at his ego. "How's the child? Brandon, isn't it?"

Percy narrowed his eyes, and Shelton braced for his next attack, but at that moment, Stewart's wife discovered

Shelton on the couch. She immediately took Nevil's spot beside him. "Darling!"

"Hi, Andrea." Shelton moved her hand from his knee, only to lift it from his thigh the next instant.

"You naughty boy. So this is where you've been hiding." Andrea leaned against him, and Shelton could smell the gin on her breath. He scrambled to his feet when she brushed his lap with her hands. He wished Andrea would try to seduce another one of her husband's gay friends at the party. Between her and Nevil, his head was reeling.

As if conjured, Nevil appeared at his side, handing Shelton a glassful of golden liquid. It smelled like bourbon. A good one. Percy's laugh dripped spite, and they both glanced at him. "I didn't know Shelton liked girls," Percy drawled, waving a hand at Andrea. Shelton grimaced, knowing Percy was trying to stir up drama. At the attention, Andrea curled her lips into a sly smile and lounged back on the couch, sipping her martini, her lascivious gaze traveling from Shelton's shoulders to his dark slacks.

Nevil looked back at Shelton. "Neither did I," he said, interested.

Before Shelton could disillusion him, someone pushed between them. The interloper threw an arm around Nevil's neck and then kissed his cheek.

"Michael!" Nevil grinned at the attractive blond. "What brings you here?"

"I'm with Sara Gibbs. And who's this gorgeous man?" Shelton blinked when he realized the guy meant him.

"This is Shelton," Nevil replied, slipping an arm around Shelton's waist. "You met him before."

"He likes girls," Percy put in nastily and raised his glass as Shelton glowered at him. The joke was quickly getting old.

"Is that so?" Michael remarked, his tone cheery in contrast. "How nice. Oh, Nevil, that reminds me..." Michael pulled Nevil aside. Shelton watched their animated conversation a moment, remembering he'd met Michael Barns at the pub with Nevil. He moved across the room to the wall, needing a sturdy prop to lean against as the last drink took effect.

Shelton floated, pleasantly dizzy, but he hadn't had enough to drink to numb the stab of jealousy when Nevil leaned over Percy's chair and whispered in his ear. Percy looked into Nevil's face and laughed, a tinge of color in his cheeks.

Seeing them together, Shelton thought of the jewelry box in his coat pocket and wished he'd had the balls earlier to give it to Nevil. He wasn't sure if he'd ever have the nerve. What if Nevil didn't want it? Irritated with himself, he made his way through the crowd to the kitchen, intent on finding the bottle of bourbon he'd seen on the counter earlier and refresh his drink.

The kitchen proved to be as crowded as the rest of the house, and Shelton brushed impatiently at his alcohol blurred eyes. Where was that damn bottle? When he found it, he nearly knocked it into the sink before pouring a good amount of the golden liquid into his glass.

He sipped the warming drink and let its slight burn trickle down his throat. He supposed Nevil couldn't help himself with those beautiful men. Until a short time ago, Nevil could have slept with any number of them. They'd only been a couple for half a year, after all.

Chapter Two

Shelton took another swallow of the numbing liquid, then looked at his glass, nearly empty again, and used both hands to set it on the countertop. It hadn't helped at all. He leaned over the sink but refused to throw up. Shelton jumped when an arm went around his shoulders, too surprised to struggle as he was dragged across the crowded kitchen and pushed through a doorway.

He squinted in the dim streetlight coming through a curtained window. Nevil slammed the door of the utility room and twisted the lock in the doorknob.

"What's the matter?" he asked, wincing at the slur in his voice. Nevil crossed to him in two strides. He shoved Shelton against the dryer and then gave him a hard, urgent kiss. Shelton turned his head away, and Nevil bit him on the lip.

"Ouch! What are you angry about?" Shelton asked, not liking the glare in Nevil's eyes.

"You deserted me," Nevil growled against his mouth. "Percy practically raped me on the couch, unable to keep his hands to himself, apparently, and you weren't even there to help. Some hero you are."

"You can handle Percy without me," Shelton asserted, then yelped as Nevil grabbed his arms. Shelton was confused when Nevil brutally kissed him, his tongue darting into Shelton's mouth. He bent Shelton back into an uncomfortable position over the dryer and continued to plunder his mouth.

Shelton struggled a little when Nevil dropped his hand to his groin. He squeezed Shelton through his slacks and gave a guttural laugh, stroking Shelton, his hold too tight to be comfortable. Damn. Nevil had never made him feel cheap like this before.

It slowly rose through his muddled brain that Nevil must be hurting and acting on it, probably from Shelton's seeming indifference to Percy's flirtations. It always surprised him to find a chink in Nevil's confidence.

Shelton pushed against Nevil, and Nevil stepped back, eyes dark with pain. Shelton placed a hand on Nevil's heaving chest. He could feel the rapid heartbeat against his palm. A tear clung to Nevil's thick lashes, and Shelton swallowed his pride. "I love you, Nevil. You're my boyfriend! I love having you all to myself and certainly don't want anyone else. Please tell me you still feel the same way."

Nevil narrowed his eyes, then hid his face against Shelton's neck. "I'm a fool. I'm sorry. Of course I only want you. It's just that I've never belonged to anyone before." He shrugged. "It makes me crazy when I think you don't care."

Shelton felt an unaccustomed thrill of power that this gorgeous, virile man picked him out of all the others. Shelton put a finger under Nevil's chin and raised his face for a tender kiss. Nevil sighed into Shelton's mouth, warm hands sliding up his back to urge him closer. Shelton gave in to Nevil willingly, molding his body against Nevil's enticing heat. Desire flared through him when Nevil ground his hardness against his hipbone.

He imagined them naked, Nevil's glorious cock twined with his in an erotic, electrifying dance, the friction of their balls making Shelton weak with pleasure.

"Let me love you," Shelton whispered, wild with the thought, but Nevil grabbed his wrists, not letting Shelton touch him.

"Not yet," Nevil murmured in Shelton's ear, trailing passionate kisses along his chin and licking the pulse in Shelton's neck.

"But Nevil…" Shelton pleaded, wanting that hot, silky shaft rubbing against his hip inside his mouth.

"No," Nevil said, then laughed and deftly undid the button and zipper of Shelton's pants.

"Nevil!" Shelton looked at the door. "If I can't—"

"Shut up." Nevil kissed him and then, with a strength that always surprised Shelton, lifted him onto the dryer. He whisked Shelton's pants and boxers below his knees.

"I don't think—" Shelton lost coherent thought as Nevil's mouth engulfed him. He had no chance. Usually, they drew out their lovemaking as long as possible, taking and giving pleasure with abandon and inventiveness. But this was too sudden. Shelton's head swam with alcohol and pleasure as Nevil sucked on him. Their intimacy couldn't be halted even when someone banged on the door.

Nevil pushed Shelton onto his back on the dryer, continuing to suck him, kneading Shelton's balls, and then sliding a finger up inside him. God! Shelton came in a few short, frenzied thrusts, feeling the muscles of Nevil's throat constrict around him as Nevil swallowed his come with a hum of wicked glee.

Bliss crept over Shelton as he stared at the flat ceiling while Nevil continued to nibble on him.

"You're too good to me," he murmured, noticing that the banging on the door had stopped. Good. It had been annoying. Nevil licked his way up Shelton's body to his lips, and Shelton gave him the slow, deep kisses that Nevil enjoyed so much.

Shelton moved his lips to Nevil's ear. "Come inside me," he urged, aching for the fulfillment of Nevil pushing into him. Nevil groaned, enfolding him in his arms and helping him sit up on the dryer.

"Not yet," Nevil whispered, though Shelton could see the arousal straining against the fly of Nevil's pants. "Good God, Shelton! I love the way those men stare at you. I know they're curious, dying to know how you keep my interest."

Nevil's eyes gleamed as his gaze traveled Shelton's body to his softened dick, and Nevil slid his hands around to caress Shelton's bare ass. "I don't dare tell them how your lovemaking intoxicates me. How the feel, and taste, and smell of you drives me wild. It excites me every day, knowing we'll spend the night together."

Shelton stared into Nevil's eyes, seeing the love there that Nevil hardly ever spoke of. Shelton's throat tightened, and he put his arms around Nevil's neck. "I love you," he said and gave Nevil a tender kiss.

A smile crossed Nevil's contented face, turning to an impish grin, and Nevil pulled Shelton to his feet and patted his bottom.

"Get dressed. We're supposed to be at a party," Nevil ordered, then turned on his heel and went to the door. Shelton scrambled to draw up his pants as Nevil flung open the door into the crowded kitchen.

"About time," someone muttered, striding past Nevil to grab an ice chest off the floor. Shelton noticed it was the girl he'd been speaking with earlier. He thought her name was Angie. The girl gave him an exaggerated wink as she dragged the chest out of the utility room.

"Let me help you." Shelton grabbed the other handle and assisted her into the living room.

Noticing how late it was getting, Shelton returned to the kitchen for a mug of the aromatic coffee someone had brewed. Time to sober up if he was going to drive home. After filling a mug, he went in search of Nevil who'd wandered off again. Finding him back on the couch, Shelton leaned against the wall, watching him. Nevil was in his element—surrounded by friends, a drink in his hand, joking with a young man sitting at his feet.

He smiled ruefully, reminding himself that Nevil's flirting never meant anything. At least Percy—the only man who shook his confidence where Nevil was concerned—had left the group. Nevil swore they'd broken off their romance, but that hadn't been Percy's idea. He had made it clear he'd sleep with Nevil again under any condition. It had been plain in every glance and smile Percy sent Nevil's way. Shelton trusted Nevil, but that didn't mean he liked having their past relationship shoved in his face.

Shelton swallowed the last of his coffee and returned to the kitchen for more, his smile indulgent when Nevil's shout of laughter reached him from the other room. It looked as though Shelton would be driving home just like he'd thought.

Someone had put on a fresh pot, and Shelton leaned on the countertop, chin in his hand as he watched the dark liquid drip into the decanter. A smile lifted his lips, body warming when he remembered the small jewelry box in his coat pocket. He began a lazy fantasy, alternately giving Nevil his gift before or maybe after making crazy love with him. Either way would be perfect.

The coffee seemed to drip even more slowly, and Shelton blinked the dream from his eyes and left the kitchen. Deciding to explore the house while he waited for the bracing beverage, he climbed the stairs to the second floor.

Sounds of laughter and sex drifted out of the closed doors of the master suite when Shelton walked along the hallway, and he shook his head. He'd seen Stewart heading for the den with a bottle of scotch earlier and wondered what poor fool Stewart's wife had lured into her bed. He knew they enjoyed an open marriage, but Shelton could never be comfortable with that lifestyle.

He wandered up the narrow stairway at the end of the hall and discovered a room little more than an attic. Leaning his forehead against the cool glass of a window, he watched the snow fall outside, illuminated by the glow from a neighbor's house. The party was winding down, and he'd be able to take Nevil home. He grinned, embarrassed at the twitch in his pants, amazed at how he could never get enough of Nevil.

He knew Nevil would eventually miss him and come looking for him, but Shelton heard the familiar steps pounding up the stairway sooner than he'd expected. A tingle of excitement ran through him as Nevil entered the room and pressed against his back, Nevil's body fittingly perfectly into his. He nuzzled Shelton's ear and dropped a bottle of lotion and a hand towel on the windowsill. "I've been searching everywhere for you. Look what I found in the bathroom."

Heat slammed through Shelton. They'd both tested negative for HIV and any other STI in their last couple of tests and had done away with condoms altogether. The thought of Nevil thrusting his naked cock into him sent the blood rushing to Shelton's groin, making his slacks uncomfortably tight.

Shelton leaned his head back against Nevil's shoulder, and Nevil gave him a hungry kiss.

"Let me make love to you," Nevil whispered, slipping his hands under Shelton's shirt. Shelton drew a quick breath as Nevil pinched his nipples, his tongue sliding in and out of Shelton's mouth. Shelton recalled that same naughty mouth on him earlier and groaned in his throat. Nevil laughed as he slid his hand into Shelton's pants and fondled his dick.

"What about the door?" Shelton managed to gasp between Nevil's kisses.

"What? Do you want me to open it farther?"

Shelton's face heated. Nevil had rooted out his fetish for making love in risqué places and delighted in teasing Shelton about it.

Chuckling, Nevil left him to nudge the door closed with his foot, then returned and removed Shelton's clothing with practiced ease. Nevil stripped out of his own clothes, but Shelton grabbed his wrist when Nevil reached for the lotion. Shelton turned in Nevil's arms to meet his questioning look.

"Not yet," Shelton teased, nipping Nevil's ear.

"Someone's bound to come looking—"

"You haven't let me touch you all night. Please, baby," Shelton said, dropping his hand to Nevil's rigid cock. "Let me suck on you just a little?"

Shelton thrilled at the flush that rose in Nevil's face. Shelton sank to his knees before Nevil could reply. He nuzzled on one of Nevil's tight balls, then the other, feverishly aroused by the heat and smell of him.

Shelton rubbed his cheek against Nevil's shaft before sliding his tongue up the beautiful erection. He nibbled on the tip, teasing himself as much as Nevil, before swallowing as much as he could. God, he loved the salty taste of his man, the silken hardness of Nevil's dick between his tongue and the roof of his mouth, choking him if he was gluttonous.

Palming Nevil's dick, Shelton pushed his hard cock in and out of his mouth. He grew further aroused by how the skin slid over the hard shaft as he stroked it. He licked the tangy, glistening precome from the head and shuddered, imagining Nevil's lips on the tip of his own dick.

Nevil jumped when they heard laughter from below and threaded his fingers through Shelton's curls, urging his head back. "We don't have time for this!" Nevil pleaded, and Shelton took pity on his anguish, knowing how he loved to be sucked.

"Whatever you say," Shelton said, giving in. He rose and braced himself against the sturdy windowpane. Nevil playfully smacked Shelton's rump, probably for his smug tone, then squeezed lotion onto his fingertips and pushed them into Shelton's ass. Shelton winced at the burn and willed his body to relax as Nevil pushed more lotion into him, then positioned himself. The initial pressure drew a grunt from him, but then Nevil slid inside, shoving deeply into his core.

He grew dizzy as Nevil continued to plunge into him, becoming lightheaded with pleasure from the amazing friction as Nevil grabbed his hips and pulled Shelton back against him with each thrust. He cried out when Nevil reached around and stroked his throbbing cock. Hard and fast, Nevil drove deeper than ever into him. As Nevil climaxed, completing him, Shelton came mindlessly in Nevil's hand.

Shelton clung to the window frame as Nevil leaned against his back, whispering endearments in his ear. His fingers roamed Shelton's body as if memorizing every line. When Nevil pulled out, Shelton faced him and laced his fingers behind his neck.

"Let's go home," he pleaded against Nevil's lips. "I don't want to share you anymore. And I'd like privacy for the things I want to do to you."

"If that's what you want," Nevil said, burrowing his face against Shelton's neck. "Our bed would feel terrific right about now."

"Oh, you won't be sleeping," Shelton assured him and lost his heart all over again as Nevil's face lit with pleasure.

They wiped up with the hand towel then helped each other dress, Nevil stealing a kiss for each button on Shelton's shirt. Shelton held Nevil's hand as they returned downstairs, eager for the coming night. In his hurry, he stumbled on the last step, embarrassed when he caught Nevil's laughing glance.

Nevil fondly touched his face. "Um, maybe I should call us a cab?" he suggested, pulling his cell phone out of a pocket.

"Probably a good idea," Shelton agreed, still feeling the effects of the drinks he'd had earlier. Nevil made the call, and then Shelton urged him to hurry as they parted in the foyer, keen to get home so he could ask Nevil his question. Nevil flashed him a grin before disappearing into the living room to say his goodbyes. Shelton retrieved his coat from the closet, pulling it on as he went to the kitchen for another mug of coffee.

Stepping outside, he sipped the scalding liquid while he waited on the porch for the cab. The snow had stopped falling, but it was still bitterly cold out. His breath made a plume of mist when he blew on the coffee to cool it. He dearly wanted to be in his warm bed, wrapped in Nevil's arms. He thought of Nevil's gift, safe in his pocket, and a smile of anticipation touched his lips. He spent the time waiting for the taxi daydreaming of Nevil's ardent responses to his question.

Hearing voices at the door, he glanced up and frowned as the young man who'd sat at Nevil's feet earlier now kissed Nevil's cheek, hand lingering on his chest. Vexed, Shelton took a step toward them, the guy's crush obvious. Nevil laughed and then crossed to meet Shelton. He threw an arm across Shelton's shoulders and gave him a sloppy kiss.

"Let's go home, love," Nevil said loudly as the taxi pulled into the driveway, playing it up for the young man's benefit. He started down the stairs and slipped on the bottom step of the porch, making a grab for the railing. Shelton put an arm around his waist and helped him to the car. He opened the door, careful that Nevil didn't bump his head getting into the backseat.

Shelton moved around the back of the taxi, brushing the loose snow from the windshield with his gloved hand, and then taking the seat behind the driver's. It was a relief to be out of the cold. He turned to Nevil, touching his knee, wanting to kiss him. He caught the driver's annoyed glance in the rearview mirror and settled back in the cushions, pulling on his seat belt.

"Take us home," Nevil commanded, sounding out of breath. A thrill shot through Shelton, and he quickly gave the driver their address. The man put the car in gear and eased on the gas, slowing immediately when the tires spun as he turned onto the road.

They began the slow drive down the mountainside, and Shelton clasped his hands, knuckles whitening as the car gained momentum on the winding road. After only a few minutes, he heard the driver swear, and his heart jumped when a blanket of freezing fog met them on a curve. Visibility reduced to no more than a car's length ahead. Ice glittered on the trees as the headlights swept over them.

The driver tapped on the brakes to slow further, and the car slid on black ice. He turned at once into the slide, but Shelton cried out as the car nevertheless began a sickening spin toward the shoulder and the drop-off into the trees. He cast a frantic look at Nevil sleeping peacefully beside him. God, it couldn't end like this!

Breathing a prayer, the driver stomped on the brake, wrenching the wheel in the opposite direction. The sedan jolted under them and slowed its spin. Not enough. Shelton watched in terror, heart in his throat, as they came closer to a tree on the side of the road. Branches filled his window, and time seemed to slow as the car spun into it. Metal screeched on impact, the door bulging toward him, and he instinctively closed his eyes as shattered glass rained over him. His seatbelt cut into his hipbones with bruising force, then broke, and he cracked his head against the window frame. Light and blinding pain shot behind his eyes, and he fell into darkness.

Shelton floated in a gray mist. He had the vague thought he was lost in the fog. But not cold. In fact... Shelton looked down. His body sat there, but he couldn't feel anything.

"Nevil?" he called, unsure. He had trouble turning his neck, then screamed as feeling returned, his head pulsing with pain. Fighting the bile in his throat, he raised a trembling hand and brushed the tears and blood from his eyes.

"Nevil?" he called again, dizzy with relief when Nevil moved in the seat beside him and sat up with a groan.

"What happened?" Nevil asked. Then his eyes widened with shock. "God, Shelton. You're bleeding. What...?" He shut his mouth with a click of teeth. Disengaging his seatbelt, he scrambled to his knees, pulling a handkerchief from a pocket.

Shelton hissed with pain as Nevil reached over and pressed the cloth to his forehead. "Ouch!"

"Don't be a baby," Nevil teased, though his voice choked on tears. "Here. Hold this in place." Shelton held the cloth to his forehead while Nevil leaned into the front seat to check the driver.

"He's unconscious," Nevil informed Shelton. Shelton heard him cursing as he pulled his cell phone from a pocket and fumbled with the buttons, talking urgently to whoever had answered.

"Emergency services said they'll have help here in ten minutes," Nevil assured him. Shelton nodded, his mind beginning to drift from the pain and shock. The night had turned icy, and he shivered. Nevil stripped out of his coat and laid it over him.

"Stay with me," Nevil pleaded. Shelton felt incredibly sleepy. He drifted off as Nevil's phone rang and then roused, still sluggish, when he heard Nevil say Percy's name. But he couldn't keep his eyes open and fell asleep with the scream of sirens ringing in his ears.

Chapter Three

Shelton woke and stared at the ceiling for several minutes, disoriented. The bedside lamp was on. Maybe he'd fallen asleep reading. No, he wasn't holding a book. And where was Nevil?

Pushing up on his elbows, he fought a wave of dizziness and gasped as memory returned. They'd been in an accident. He remembered sirens...

"Nevil!" he shouted, anxious, and winced at a spike of pain in his head. *Where is Nevil?* Getting no reply, Shelton gingerly sat up and swung his feet over the bed. He stood, touching the bandage on his aching forehead. He must have hit the window frame pretty hard. Not feeling any other injuries on his body, he left the room, desperate to check on Nevil.

Shelton stopped in disbelief as he turned the corner of the hallway and then took a step back into the shadows. Common sense said not to watch, but he stood his ground, riveted, as Percy wrapped his arms around Nevil. Nevil pressed his face into Percy's shoulder, and Percy stroked the dark hair that Shelton delighted in threading his fingers through as Nevil and he made love.

Percy raised Nevil's chin, and Shelton went back to the empty bedroom and sat on the edge of the bed, trembling when he heard the front door close and footsteps come down the hallway.

"Good. You're awake," Nevil said, cheerful as he came into the room. He sat next to Shelton and touched the large bandage on Shelton's forehead with care. "You've stopped bleeding, thank goodness." He tilted Shelton's chin to look him in the eyes. "Last night at the hospital, the doctors said you had a slight concussion but that I could take you home if I kept an eye on you. You've slept most of today away. Well, when I wasn't waking you up to check on you. You don't remember that? Okay, I'm babbling. How do you feel?"

Shelton swallowed the lump in his throat. God, he didn't even remember being taken to the emergency room.

"Okay, I guess. Tired."

An off tone in his voice must have reached Nevil. "What's wrong?"

"When were you going to tell me about Percy?"

"Tell you what about Percy?"

Shelton didn't reply, and Nevil rose and moved across the room to lean against the dresser, arms crossed. "You saw me kiss him. It didn't mean what you think." Nevil snorted when Shelton kept silent. His eyes narrowed to turquoise sparks. "What are you thinking?"

"I think I deserve an explanation."

Nevil straightened from the dresser, and Shelton jumped at the anger in his voice. "I had a shock last night, and Percy was being a friend. It would be nice if you trusted me—" The phone in Nevil's pocket chimed, and Nevil drew it out, cursing under his breath when he looked at the screen. "I have to go. The taxi's here to take me back to Stewart's for the car." Nevil jammed the phone in his pocket and flicked a glance at Shelton. "We'll finish this discussion later."

Shelton watched, numb, as Nevil stormed from the room and flinched when the front door slammed. Damn. He slid to his feet, ignoring the dizziness as he hurried to the foyer. Realizing he wore only his briefs he paused, hand on the doorknob, but then flung the door open anyway. Hoping to catch Nevil before he drove away, he had to come to an abrupt stop to keep from colliding with Nevil in the doorway.

"Forgot the keys." Nevil mumbled. He pushed by Shelton into the living room and snatched the key ring from the coffee table.

"Nevil, stay and talk to me," Shelton urged as Nevil stormed back to the front door.

Nevil stopped but kept his face averted, still angry. "We've been together for what, six months? If you don't trust me by now—" He broke off and reached for the door.

"Nevil," Shelton said, his voice raw. "Drive carefully."

Nevil glanced at Shelton, and his expression softened, though the anger didn't completely leave his eyes. Nevil touched Shelton's hand. "I'll be back in a bit. Don't worry, I'll be careful. We'll talk later."

He kissed Shelton's cheek and disappeared out the door. Shelton waited in the foyer, hoping Nevil would come back. When he heard the car's engine rumble, then fade into the distance, Shelton went into the living room and dropped onto the couch. He buried his face in his hands. Why did he always have to fling his insecurities in Nevil's face?

"But did you have to kiss Percy?" Shelton asked the empty room since Nevil wasn't there. He admitted to himself that Nevil's ex remained a sore spot.

Restless, Shelton got to his feet and paced the apartment. Time dragged as he waited for Nevil to return. "Oh hell," he muttered and went to the bedroom to dress. He pulled on his boots, then grabbed his coat and scarf and set the snow cap over his ears, careful of the bandage on his forehead. Opening the front door, he drew on his gloves. Snow drifted up against the brownstone, but the steps and walkway had been cleared. Shelton made his way to the sidewalk, careful of the ice. It had stopped snowing, but the sky looked gray and heavy, promising more.

It's only two blocks to the coffee shop, and I'll be back before Nevil even knows I'm gone. Shelton tried to ignore his niggling conscience as he walked along the shoveled sidewalk. He knew it was stupid to be out in this weather, but he felt too wound up to stay indoors. Besides, the fresh air would clear his head.

The afternoon proved colder than he'd thought it would be, slicing like a knife into his lungs. A sheet of ice covered the ground, and Shelton shivered long before he crossed the street to the second block of buildings. The coffee shop sat at the far end of a long row of department stores, all of which seemed to be closed. He walked faster, afraid he'd find the coffee shop closed as well.

He let out a relieved breath when he spied its welcoming light spilling onto the street. By this time, his hands and feet had grown numb, and his head pounded. He pushed through the doors and stumbled to the nearest table as the wave of heat in the building made him dizzy.

It took a minute for the lightheadedness to pass. Shelton became aware of someone speaking at his elbow and raised his head to give the impatient waiter his order, noticing there were few other customers in the shop as he shrugged out of his coat. He stared, dismayed, when he recognized the wide, smoky gray eyes watching him from across the room.

Percy picked up his drink and joined Shelton, pulling out a chair opposite him as the waiter brought Shelton his macchiato. The young man shoved several napkins into Shelton's hands. "You're bleeding," he said, concerned, and gestured to Shelton's head.

Shelton touched the bandage and stared at the blood on his fingers. No wonder his head hurt, the pain intense.

"Here. Let me." Percy plucked a napkin from his hand and dabbed gently at Shelton's forehead. "It's not bad. The cold probably opened up the wound." They both glanced out the windows at the falling snow, lit by the coffee shop's lights. Percy looked back at Shelton and asked with an edge in his voice, "What are you doing out here, anyway? Thought you had a concussion?"

Shelton shrugged, seeing no need to explain himself to Percy. He braced, though, when Percy narrowed his eyes similar to the way Nevil did when angry. But then Percy's expression changed, and Shelton blinked several times at the rueful grin that touched his rival's face.

"I want to hate you, Shelton," Percy confessed. "But the more I see of you, the more I understand Nevil's enchantment."

Shelton gaped, not knowing what to say or think of that statement, delivered with sincerity.

Percy put his hands out in a conciliatory gesture. "Don't take it the wrong way. I wouldn't dream of coming between you and Nevil. In fact, I saw Nevil earlier today and apologized for my behavior at the party. After hearing him on the phone last night... He was crying when you wouldn't wake up. God, Shelton, that man loves you."

"I know," Shelton replied. The warmth of the room took its toll, and he knuckled his eyes as a sleepy feeling stole over him.

Percy gave him a close look and then shook his arm, drawing his attention. "Don't fall asleep. What was I saying? Oh yes, how adorable you are." He laughed at Shelton's expression. "You should see yourself, face all soft and dreamy. What man wouldn't want to wake up to that and kiss you into a delirium of bliss?"

Shelton sputtered, knowing he should be offended, but his head hurt, and Percy was teasing him anyway. He frowned at his next thought. "I saw Nevil kissing you today," he said and bit his lip, appalled to be discussing it with him.

Percy shook his head. "Put it out of your mind. It was a goodbye kiss between old friends. After seeing Nevil with you at the party last night and his concern today, I realize I'm wasting my time. We never shared what the two of you have together. I won't be bothering you anymore."

"Oh. Okay," Shelton said, wishing his head would stop pounding. He had a hard time following what Percy was saying. "What time is it?" he asked in sudden concern, afraid he'd stayed too long, and Nevil would get home before he did. He climbed to his feet but paused halfway, unsteady and confused by his weakness.

Percy leaned across the table and pressed him down into the chair. "I'll give you a ride. Put your coat on first. Wait, never mind." Percy shoved back his chair and stood.

Shelton followed his gaze to the entrance. Nevil stood poised in the doorway, dark hair standing awry as if he'd jammed his fingers through it. His eyes blazed with fury; Shelton could hardly catch his breath at their beauty.

"I kept him awake, but you better get him home," Percy said when Nevil swept up to them.

"That's my intention. Shelton, what the hell do you—" He broke off, his grip painful on Shelton's arm. "Get your coat on. We're leaving."

"Nevil—"

"Now!" Nevil growled.

Shelton couldn't remember the last time Nevil had been so angry with him. Well, except for last night at the party, but that had been a misunderstanding. He hurried to pull on his coat and gloves before winding the scarf quickly around his neck. He shot Percy a look, but Nevil's snarl sent him scurrying from the coffee shop without another word.

Shelton climbed into the passenger seat of their car and rested his head back on the cushion. The quick change in temperature from the warm shop to the near-freezing storm had intensified his pain, the pounding in his head so fierce he hardly noticed when Nevil started the car and drove home.

Nevil wouldn't look at him as he helped him from the car into the house. Silently removing Shelton's coat and gloves, he then pushed him into the chair by the door to remove his boots.

"Nevil..." Shelton began, shutting his mouth at Nevil's glare. Nevil disposed of his own coat and boots, took Shelton by the arm and marched him into the living room, and shoved him down on the couch. Nevil stood over him for a second and then knelt to rub Shelton's numb feet. Shelton watched the top of Nevil's dark head, and hot tears filled his eyes.

"I'm sorry," he said, throat so choked with tears it came out as a whisper.

Nevil's gaze swept up to him, angry, but then his face crumpled, and Nevil laid his head in Shelton's lap. Shelton had to strain to hear his mumbled words. "After the accident, when you wouldn't wake up... I had to sit in that damn car waiting for the ambulance, thinking you were dying." Nevil drew a hard breath. "Then today you go tramping through the city in a blizzard. God..."

Shelton twined his fingers through Nevil's hair. "I'm sorry. My head hurts," he said in a small voice, bewildered as the pain became a knife behind his eyes.

Nevil raised his head from Shelton's lap, wiping his eyes. "I'd better change the bandage. It might hurt," he said wretchedly and lifted the cap from Shelton's head. He fumbled with the prescription bottle on the end table. "Here, take these."

Shelton opened his mouth when Nevil pressed two pills between his lips, then took a sip of water. He felt warmth in his stomach, which spread to the rest of his body, easing the pain to a dull, manageable throb.

"Nice," he murmured as Nevil finished with the bandage. Shelton heard Nevil's faint chuckle, and then he sat beside Shelton and gave him a long, adoring kiss, making Shelton feel enjoyably dizzy.

Nevil picked up an item from the end table and held out the small jewelry box Shelton had been carrying around the day before. "I found this in your coat when I was gathering things for the dry cleaners."

Shelton stared numbly at the box and then hid his face in his hands, self-conscious and embarrassed. This wasn't how he'd planned things at all. "Can you just forget about it? It was a stupid idea. I shouldn't have—"

Nevil's lips were warm on his, stilling Shelton's protest. He caressed Shelton's cheek with his thumb, wiping away a tear. "Is it for me?"

Shelton bobbed his head once, his gaze intent on Nevil's face as he opened the box. Nevil's hand froze, and Shelton grew anxious at his continued silence. At last, Nevil turned his head to meet Shelton's stare. Shelton saw the tears clinging to his dark lashes and the happiness swimming in his eyes. Nevil asked him in complete earnestness, "Are you sure?"

Shelton nodded, his throat too constricted to speak. Nevil made a pleased sound as he took the white gold band from its cushion. He traced the Celtic knot with a finger. Watching him, Shelton took a breath for courage. "I love you, Nevil. It's my promise to stay faithful to you."

"It's lovely, and I'll wear it because I love you too." Nevil slipped the ring on his left hand, next to the small ruby Nevil's mother had given him years ago before she and his father had been killed in a car accident. He brought the ring to his lips, then took Shelton's hands in his and squeezed them gently. "Thank you. And Shelton, after last night, when I thought I might lose you... I can't imagine ever wanting to be with anyone but you for the rest of my life."

Shelton mumbled words of love, wanting to respond to the flash in Nevil's eyes, but the pain medication made him wonderfully drowsy. Nevil laughed and eased Shelton to his feet. "Come to bed, love. This time I'll make sure you stay there."

Nevil took his hand and led Shelton into the bedroom. Tingling as Nevil undressed him, Shelton felt safe but faintly detached from his body as they slid between the sheets. He didn't know what the doctor had prescribed for him, but he liked it, the pain in his head a thing of the past. Nevil's sleek body against him and the intoxicating kisses became everything.

Shelton made a vague protest when Nevil rained little kisses over his face. "I'm very sleepy, Nevil. I can't—"

Nevil's lips covered his again, tasting him, and Shelton lost his train of thought.

"Don't do anything," Nevil murmured in Shelton's ear before sucking on his earlobe. "I swear to God, I thought you were dying last night. I need to be with you, hold you safe in my arms, and make love to you. Ignore me if you want to. Fall asleep. I'll try not to disturb you."

Shelton felt his bones dissolve at Nevil's words, and he sank into the mattress, teetering in bliss on the border between wakefulness and sleep. Nevil kissed him repeatedly—sensuous kisses that sent a wave of heat through him. Shelton tried to lift his hand, but the effort proved beyond him.

Nevil took his time, licking Shelton's chest, kissing his nipples. The mobile lips brushed along Shelton's body, down one leg and up the other. Shelton felt sure Nevil had tasted every inch of him before stopping to nuzzle Shelton's balls. Fire had followed Nevil's tongue, and Shelton lost his air when Nevil took Shelton's dick into his mouth.

He choked on a whimper. Nevil sucked him with exquisite slowness, lips sliding up his shaft, nursing on the end of him, drawing out Shelton's pleasure. Skilled torture. Shelton's orgasm started in his toes—a wonderful tingle that flowed up his legs, pooled in his stomach, swarmed in his cock, and spilled into Nevil's mouth in one glorious wave.

When he came down gently from his orgasm, he found Nevil lying beside him, watching him.

"I love you," Nevil whispered against Shelton's ear, a tremor in his voice. The heat from his body wrapped Shelton in a safe cocoon, and Shelton met his gaze. "So... who's this fascinating man you promised not to have an affair with?"

"What?" Shelton sputtered. He hadn't meant... He let out an exasperated sigh at the amusement in Nevil's face. "You know there's no one but you, Nevil."

"I know." Nevil kissed his cheek. "And you're everything I desire. You have my heart. Go to sleep, love. I'll keep you safe." He pulled Shelton close.

Shelton drew a deep, contented breath. "Good night, Nevil," he murmured, his heart overflowing with joy as he took Nevil's goodnight kiss with him into his dreams.

SHELTON'S

CHOICE

Chapter One

"Have you told him yet?"

"Hmm?" Shelton murmured, reluctant to put down the book he was reading. Only a few pages remained to the thriller, and he still hadn't a clue who the killer would turn out to be.

"Have you told your tall, dark, and wickedly handsome boyfriend that you're leaving?"

Shelton shot the man at his elbow an irritated glance. "What do you want, Ted?" He noticed the coffee shop filling up and hoped his coworker wouldn't take the vacant chair at his table. Ted Pringle was personable enough, even attractive in a light blond, pale blue-eyed way. He also gossiped, though, and lived to stir up trouble, in and out of the office.

Ted threw his hands up. "Hey, I was only asking. We'll be going in a few months, and—"

"Leave me alone." Shelton turned back to his book and skimmed the page to find his place. Ted touched his arm, and Shelton spun on him but swallowed his angry words. Ted's attention wasn't on him. He looked across the room, a smile of triumph on his lips.

Shelton followed Ted's gaze, and his heart jumped, then settled into a delighted patter. Nevil stood in the doorway of the coffee shop, scanning the tables with his beautiful turquoise eyes. Wickedly handsome? Damn right he was. Even after a year together, Nevil's smile still had the power to melt his bones and leave him weak with want.

Nevil spotted him, and Shelton waved the book. A curious expression passed over Nevil's face as he approached his table, and Shelton remembered Ted's hand on his arm. He pulled free, and Ted chuckled, his breath warm in Shelton's ear when he bent down and whispered, "Don't forget to tell him."

Shelton grumbled and then forgot all about Ted when Nevil stopped at the table, his eyes dancing with mischief.

"What are you doing here? Sit down," Shelton babbled, feeling the warmth of a blush on his cheeks as Nevil watched Ted's retreating back as he headed for the coffee bar.

"Okay, but only for a minute. I have a surprise for you, and I've already wasted enough time tracking you down. Off work early?" Nevil took the empty chair Shelton had motioned to and leaned across the table. A teasing smile covered his face. "I may have to blindfold you."

Heat swept through Shelton at the ardent look in Nevil's eyes. God, he wanted Nevil to take him right there at the table. He agonized under the constraint of public opinion that kept him from kissing Nevil's smiling lips.

Nevil settled back into his chair. "Who was that?" he asked, nodding toward the crowd at the coffee bar.

"Just that annoying prick from Accounts I told you about."

"Gossiping Ted? What did he say? I wanted to smack his pretty face for standing so close to you."

"I'm sure he wanted to make you jealous, as if he ever could. So, about this blindfold..."

Nevil smiled and licked his lips, his expression provocative. "You'll see," he teased and rose to his feet. "Come on, love, before I change my mind."

Shelton kept at Nevil's heels as he wove his way through the boisterous lunch crowd to the front entrance and on to the car parked at the curb. Nevil kissed his cheek when Shelton climbed into the passenger seat of the Prius, and Shelton's heart fluttered. Nevil rarely displayed his affection in public, a sure sign he felt as aroused as Shelton did. Shelton didn't speak while Nevil slid behind the wheel and drove through the afternoon traffic, his body tingling in anticipation of their lovemaking.

"What about this blindfold?" he asked, becoming breathless at the thought. Nevil could be creative in the extreme.

"That's for later, my dear, when I have you alone and enthralled."

Shelton snorted and enjoyed Nevil's easy laughter. Grateful to be Nevil's friend as well as his lover, Shelton's spirits soared. His days filled with laughter and comradeship. He thrust Ted's stinging reminder from his mind. He'd keep that discussion for another day and take this precious time with Nevil.

Nevil skirted the city, and Shelton sat up when he took one of the smaller highways toward the mountains. "Where are we going?"

"You'll see. We put the last nail in Bill Stanton's place this morning, two weeks ahead of schedule, and Barker has given us the weekend off with a bonus." Nevil patted his pocket.

"It's only Thursday," Shelton commented.

Nevil waved it off. "I'm sure you'll come down with a cold or similar ailment by morning. Live a little, Shelton! The bank won't fall apart without you tomorrow. I want to celebrate."

Shelton leaned back in his seat. Who was he to argue? Especially when Nevil's gaze raked over him with the promise of passion in his beautiful eyes. The highway ascended steadily into the mountains, and in time, Nevil turned off along a narrow road and then onto a private driveway. Shelton whistled with approval when they pulled up to a modern glass-and-redwood-sided bungalow snug against the lake.

"It's beautiful," he said in admiration, recalling the blueprints for the house on Nevil's desk last winter.

"The Gordans haven't moved in yet and lent it to me for the weekend."

"But why?"

Nevil turned off the engine and moved closer to Shelton. "I told them it was my first-year anniversary with the man I love."

Shelton reached out and cupped the back of Nevil's head, pulling him closer for a kiss. So delicious. He never tired of the taste of this man in his arms. Nevil pressed against him, and the heat of his body ignited Shelton, the scent of Nevil's skin filling him with the longing to run his tongue over every inch of him.

Nevil groaned low in his throat and reluctantly pulled away. "Let's go inside," he said unsteadily.

"Absolutely."

They left the car, and Nevil squeezed his hand, Shelton's heart pounding with excitement as they climbed onto the wide porch surrounding the house. Nevil fished the keys from a pocket and opened the door. He waved Shelton in and hardly let the door close behind them before pulling Shelton tight against his body.

The dark head bent to him. "I love you," Nevil told him and captured Shelton's lips before he could reply. He opened to Nevil's tender assault, tasting him, their tongues twining in their own erotic dance. A flutter began in Shelton's stomach and descended to his groin. He recalled those same fantastic lips there, and his body burst to life. He hardened as Nevil plundered his mouth with kisses that scorched his blood.

He groped for the zipper of Nevil's trousers, but Nevil broke off their kiss and caught his wrist. Shelton waited, aroused and aching, as Nevil pulled a slip of black silk from a pocket.

"Close your eyes."

Shelton obediently shut his eyes, and Nevil tied the cloth around him with deft fingers, shutting out all light. He shivered, feeling Nevil's warm breath on his cheek. He turned his head and licked the heated, salty skin of Nevil's neck. Putting his mouth on the strong pulse beating there, he felt the rush of blood beneath the skin.

Nevil slipped an arm around Shelton's waist and guided him across the smooth floor. A door flung open, and then Shelton felt the thick carpet of another room under his feet as Nevil led him forward.

Nevil stopped again, and Shelton waited, keen for him to break the tension humming along his nerves. He jumped when Nevil licked his lips and teased his mouth open. Nevil kissed him lazily, tantalizing him, drawing out Shelton's expectancy to a fine point.

"Please," he panted when he thought his nerves would shatter. Nevil laughed, sounding pleased as he undressed Shelton. Shelton's body screamed for Nevil to grab his cock, but he kept silent, knowing their lovemaking became intense when he allowed Nevil to have his way.

He moaned when fingers brushed along his straining length and tickled his sac, and then light exploded in his head as Nevil rolled his balls in his hand. Nevil kissed him; hungry for more, Shelton pulled him closer, but Nevil eased away.

"None of that. In fact..." Nevil put a hand on his chest and gently pushed back. "On the bed, love."

Shelton felt the edge of the bed against his knees and sat down. The sheets were slick and cool against his skin, and he lay back, finding the pillows. Goose bumps covered his body when Nevil joined him, and his pulse raced, the anticipation driving him to distraction.

Nevil placed Shelton's arms over his head, and Shelton scrunched his face in a frown when he wound a second cloth around his wrists. "I don't think—"

"I won't hurt you," Nevil assured him as he secured Shelton's wrists to the headboard. "Quite the opposite, in fact."

What is he planning? Shelton felt vulnerable, even more so when Nevil slipped the pillow from under his head and nudged it under his lower back, lifting his butt off the mattress.

"What's that?" he asked sharply when a soft burr filled the room and then bit his lip. He knew that sound. He'd been mesmerized the times he'd watched Nevil use one. He'd even participated a time or two, holding Nevil's shuddering body in his arms as Nevil came with a shout of abandoned pleasure.

He'd been hesitant to try it himself, though. He sighed, embarrassed by his timidity. Nevil caressed his hot face and leaned close for a sweet kiss.

"You're such a delight to make love to," Nevil murmured as if reading his thoughts. "Trust me. This'll blow your mind."

Shelton drew in a lungful of air and let it out slowly, relaxing his muscles. He heard a click, and the humming of the vibrator stopped. Nevil's quick breathing filled the room, and Shelton smiled at the sound of his excitement.

"Now where did I put the lube...? Oh, yes."

Nevil moved on the bed, and Shelton heard him fumble with the nightstand. The mattress sagged again, and Shelton held his breath while Nevil blew cool air over his cock, hard and ready for their games.

"God, Nevil," he groaned as Nevil continued to tease him, flicking his tongue along his aching shaft. He cried out in surprise when Nevil licked the tip. Slippery fingers pushed against his hole and slid inside him. Shelton winced slightly at the initial pain, then squirmed when Nevil stroked the sensitive tissue, sure he would like what was coming.

The fingers withdrew, and Shelton caught his bottom lip with his teeth as he felt a strange pressure against his hole—not unpleasant, just different. Nevil must have used plenty of lubricant, because there was little resistance as he carefully inserted the head. A tingle spread through him as Nevil pushed the vibrator in deeper, slowly stretching him, creating little ripples of pleasure.

Nevil slid the device in and out several times, then rotated it. *God!* "Nevil! I can't..."

"I think we found the spot," Nevil murmured gleefully. "Do you like it there?"

"I don't..." Shelton groaned loudly, arching his back as Nevil nudged the vibrator in farther, then turned it on.

Intense pleasure swamped Shelton's senses.

"A little faster?" Nevil urged, his voice sounding thick. Shelton tossed his head. "I don't know."

Nevil made an adjustment, and a feeling bordering on ecstasy burst in Shelton's brain. He couldn't think as waves of bliss danced along his nerves.

"Nevil," he whimpered as his balls tightened, the pressure building toward climax. His body twitched, and he pushed his hips downward against the vibrator. He cried out, on the verge of coming, the exquisite pleasure of the vibrator approaching painful against his prostate.

Then Nevil's hot mouth engulfed his dick in wet heat, and it was all over. Shelton came in one quick thrust, his hips rising off the pillow. The orgasm went on and on, shattering him. He panicked a little as a buzzing grew in his head. His lips tingled, then went numb.

"Take a breath, dear."

Shelton let go of a held breath and drew delicious air into his lungs. He grinned as Nevil slipped the vibrator out and untied his hands. He felt amazing and settled into the mattress with a sigh, his body twitching as it recovered from the intense orgasm.

Nevil laughed and removed the scarf from Shelton's eyes. Shelton caught his breath at the fire in the turquoise gaze, knowing Nevil wanted him more than ever. He hooked an arm around Nevil's neck and kissed him lovingly.

"Thank you," he murmured.

A wicked smile touched Nevil's lips. "There's a way you can thank me." He smirked and guided Shelton's hand to his sleek erection. Shelton took hold of it and saw the flush of desire that crossed Nevil's face. They kissed. Then Nevil drew back and asked teasingly, "Can I get inside you now, or was your new friend enough?"

In answer, Shelton pushed him onto his back and straddled him, elated they'd forgone condoms long ago. Nevil's cock slid in easily, and Shelton groaned, more sensitive than ever. Nevil sat up, going deeper into Shelton's body. Shelton wrapped his arms around Nevil as they rocked together, the familiar joy of their lovemaking building inside him. The vibrator had been incredible but nothing like this living, flesh-and-blood man in his arms inside him, filling him with love.

Chapter Two

Shelton lingered in the shower after Nevil had climbed out, enjoying the hot spray. He sighed as his muscles relaxed, easing the soreness of his ass from their games. When the water cooled, he turned off the faucet and went in search of clothing. Nevil had packed a suitcase for them, and Shelton found a pair of worn, comfortable shorts. After slipping them on, he made his way through the house to the kitchen, admiring the contrast of dark wood floors and cream-colored walls. The modern decor went well with the understated luxury of the floor plan.

The brown-and-blue kitchen tiles felt cool against his feet as he crossed to the glass doors leading to the deck. Nevil stood over a smoking barbecue grill and waved the spatula at him.

"Smells good," Shelton said. They dallied over a kiss, and then Nevil motioned across the deck.

"Sit in the hot tub, if you want. The chicken needs a few more minutes."

Shelton eyed the sparkling water with interest. "Did you bring swimming trunks?"

"Go naked. I won't peek," Nevil teased when Shelton hesitated. Shelton playfully turned his back and slipped off his shorts, swaying his hips on the walk across the cedar decking to the hot tub. He enjoyed Nevil's admiring whistle as he climbed the few steps and eased into the deliciously hot water. His dick bobbed a second on top before sinking, and Shelton felt a twinge of regret. Nevil made it clear that the unsightly scars and dark patches of skin on Shelton's cock didn't bother him, but in moments like this, Shelton wished he was beautiful.

He laid his head back on the edge of the tub and let the jets of water massage his body. Pine trees grew to the edge of the deck, spicing the air, and the evening sun glittered on the lake. Shelton drew a contented breath and threw off his worries. He didn't want to be anywhere else in the world.

Nevil came over and sat beside him on the decking, handing him a bottle of beer.

"This is ideal, Nevil. Thank you." Shelton took a swallow of the amber liquid and handed the bottle back. Nevil put it down and slipped his feet into the water. They sat in companionable silence, Nevil twining his fingers in Shelton's curls.

He tugged gently and gave Shelton a light kiss when he looked up. "I thought you'd like this. In fact, I've been thinking of buying some property along the lake for us."

Panic churned in Shelton's stomach. It was time to tell Nevil his plans. He'd wanted to wait for the right moment. Damn it.

Nevil narrowed his eyes. "You look extremely serious all of a sudden. What is it?"

Just then the timer Nevil had set beside the grill went off, saving Shelton from answering. Nevil climbed to his feet and held out a hand. "Let's eat. I'm starving."

While Shelton dried off and slipped back into his shorts, Nevil flipped the chicken breasts one more time and placed them on a platter on the patio table he'd set earlier. He then fetched salad and a bottle of wine from a nearby cooler and sat down while Shelton quickly washed up in the kitchen. He took the chair opposite Nevil and stared at the golden chicken on his plate, his appetite lost, knowing he couldn't put off telling Nevil the truth any longer.

Nevil put his fork down. "Something's bothering you. Tell me."

Where to begin? Shelton ran a hand through his hair as he struggled for the words. He wanted this to go right. "I was offered a promotion."

"That's great. But...?" Nevil prompted when Shelton sounded anything but happy.

"It's for the branch office in Denver. I'd be a level three administrative assistant."

For a second, fear showed in the beautiful eyes fixed on him. Then Nevil blinked, and the emotion disappeared. "Colorado?"

"At the newly opened bank. They need help getting started."

"How long would you be gone? A month? Six?"

"The contract is for three years with a hefty salary increase. Nevil, come with me. With that kind of money, it wouldn't be long before you could start your own business."

Nevil shifted in his chair and crossed his arms over his chest. "It's not that simple. Do you know how many years it took us to make the connections we have here? If

I left the firm, I'd have to start from scratch, attach myself to another architectural company and begin all over again."

Shelton opened his mouth then shut it with a click of his teeth. He hadn't thought of connections. Nevil had only ever spoken of the lack of funds that kept him from opening a private business.

"I want you to come anyway," he said when he realized he had no arguments with which to persuade Nevil.

"And I think you should stay here with me, where you belong."

"If I don't take the position, they'll pass me over for Andrew Blake. If they do that, I can kiss any hope of advancement goodbye."

"Stay anyway. Let that bastard Andrew take the job. His enormous ego needs the stroking. We'd get by."

A band of steel tightened around Shelton's chest, making it painful to breathe. He shivered, not wanting to speak his next words. This wasn't how he'd planned things at all. He'd thought Nevil would be happy for him and excited to go to Denver. He bit hard on his lip, the pain easing the pressure around his heart. "I've already given them a tentative yes. I want to go."

Nevil looked stunned. "Without talking to me first? Don't I—" He stopped, and Shelton saw him swallow convulsively. "When would you leave?"

"Not until September. They won't be set up until then."

Nevil nodded and turned his head toward the water, but not before Shelton saw a gleam of tears in his eyes.

"Nevil..."

Nevil held up his hand, stopping Shelton's words. "If you've decided to go, I can't stop you. I'm disappointed that you didn't discuss this with me first before giving your answer."

Shelton sprang out of his chair and knelt beside Nevil's chair. He put a hand on Nevil's thigh, needing to touch him. "I can still tell them I changed my mind, if you're really set against this. But it's only for three years. Can't you—"

"Barker's retiring in a couple years, and I'll be made a full partner with his son. I can't leave."

Shelton looked at his hand on Nevil's bare leg, feeling the warmth of his skin. He knew its taste and how the fine hairs tickled his tongue. His enticing scent filled Shelton with sorrow, and he pushed his burning eyes against Nevil's hip. He wanted to start the day over. He wished he'd never been offered the job tempting him away from everything he loved.

Nevil tangled his fingers in Shelton's curls, emphasizing all he would lose. "What would happen if you told them no thank you?"

Shelton shrugged, gutted. "I could, but like I said, it would ruin my chances for any future promotions at the bank. And if I left the company, who'd hire me after that?"

"Fuck."

Shelton lifted his head, but Nevil gazed across the lake, and Shelton couldn't see his expression. He climbed to his feet and returned to his chair. "I've worked hard for this, Nevil. You know that. I would like to go."

"And I'm staying. Looks like we've hit an impasse."

"Can't we find a way to make this work?"

Nevil remained silent, and Shelton ate his tasteless meal with a tight throat, giving Nevil the space he obviously needed.

*

The evening remained strained between them, with Nevil drinking more than his share of the wine and answering Shelton's attempts at conversation with one-syllable replies. He'd gone inside as soon as it was dark, not even saying good night.

Shelton followed him and stood beside the bed, chewing his lips when Nevil crawled under the sheets and lay staring at the ceiling. Shelton sighed, took off his clothes, and climbed in beside him.

He stroked Nevil's arm in the faint light from the clock on the nightstand. The muscles were as tight as granite.

"Can't we talk about this?"

"We did talk about it. You want to leave. The end."

Shelton slid his hand over Nevil's chest, aching to be pulled into those strong arms and comforted. "We can—"

Nevil caught his wrist in a painful grip. "What, Shelton? Fuck? Would that make everything better? Fine." He gave Shelton a hard kiss, then flipped him to his stomach without warning and pinned him.

"Is this what you want?" Nevil growled in his ear. Shelton nodded, his heart racing, hoping the intimacy would cool Nevil's temper.

Nevil grabbed up the lubricant and entered him with minimal preparation, and Shelton pushed his face into the pillows, Nevil's lovemaking hard and quick, having nothing to do with love and everything to do with anger. He circled Shelton's nipples with his fingers, pinching roughly, plucking his nerves. He stroked down his ribs ruthlessly and rolled his aching balls.

Shelton leaked precome when Nevil palmed his dick but concentrated to stop the orgasm. Apparently, Nevil wasn't ready to forgive him, and he didn't want to come when his heart was hurting. He winced and blinked away a few scalding tears when Nevil laughed harshly, betraying his own pain. Nevil quickened his movements, his jabbing shaft plunging deeper with each stroke until Shelton's control broke. With a cry, he came in Nevil's hand. Nevil's triumphant groan heralded his own release as he pumped his semen into Shelton's body.

When Nevil's movements slowed, Shelton eased into the mattress, lonely and missing Nevil's words of love in his ear. He jumped violently when the strident notes of a synthpop song shattered the silence. Withdrawing from him, Nevil reached for his cell phone on the nightstand as the ringtone played again. "What?" he asked brusquely.

Shelton rolled over and stared at the ceiling while Nevil continued to listen to whoever was on the other end of the conversation. He glanced over when Nevil made a sputtering sound. Even in the dim light, Shelton could see the temper on his face.

Nevil yelled an obscenity into the phone and hurtled it across the room, and Shelton put a hand on his thigh. "What is it?"

Nevil growled in his throat and shoved Shelton's hand away. "That was Ted Pringle from your office. Apparently, your phone's off. Seems they need you at work early tomorrow. Change of plans. You leave for Colorado next weekend."

"Nevil—"

"Go to sleep," Nevil snapped. He climbed under the blankets and, for the first time, turned his back on Shelton. Shelton trembled in the darkness, hurting. Although Nevil lay there beside him, he already felt the hundreds of miles between them.

Chapter Three

Nevil continued to ignore him on the drive to the bank the next morning, and Shelton took a frustrated breath. Damn. Nevil hadn't spoken to him during breakfast either. Shelton wanted to know his plans. Nevil had left his clothes at the lake house, so apparently, he wouldn't be coming home any time soon.

He chewed his lips as Nevil stopped the Prius in front of the bank. There must be the right words he could say to make things right between them.

"I'll drop your suitcase at the house," Nevil said coolly, looking straight ahead through the windshield.

Shelton put a tentative hand on Nevil's knee, longing for his morning kiss. "I'm sorry. How many more times can I say it? We need to talk about this…"

Nevil glanced pointedly at his watch. "You're going to be late."

Shelton blinked at the snub, pain settling around his heart. "Goodbye," he mumbled and flung open his door. He'd barely closed it behind him before Nevil left with a squeal of tires. Shelton watched until his taillights disappeared into traffic and then entered the bank, making his way to the conference room and taking the seat closest to the door. Hopefully, it would be a short meeting and he could go home.

No such luck. Shelton rubbed his tired eyes as the meeting droned on into the afternoon and glanced at his watch when the other members of his team finally gathered their papers and left. Two o'clock, with only a few nibbles of a dry sandwich for lunch.

He stuffed paperwork into his briefcase. Plans were moving quickly in Denver. So what? What did he care when his life was in shambles? Maybe he shouldn't go to Colorado... But he deserved this promotion, dammit. His throat tightened, and he cleared it, impatient with his runaway emotions. He had to get a hold of himself.

"Everything all right?"

He glanced up on hearing the voice and nodded to the speaker. "Andrew."

"Ted said your boyfriend looked furious when he dropped you off this morning. Do you want me to talk to him? I can explain the situation. See if I can get him to understand your position."

Shelton gave him a keen look. Andrew Blake was remarkably attractive with dark hair and eyes, wide shoulders, a slim waist, and deliciously full lips. Supremely confident. No. He wasn't going anywhere near Nevil.

"Don't worry about it," he said and picked up his briefcase. He took a step but stopped in surprise when Andrew put a hand on his shoulder. He met the dark glance, and unexpected heat flushed through him at the gleam in his rich brown eyes.

Andrew leaned close, and the hint of expensive cologne teased Shelton's senses. He exhaled against Shelton's cheek, his breath warm on his skin. "Lovers can be so difficult. If you need someone to talk to, we could meet somewhere…"

Shelton blinked, a trifle shocked as Andrew's words trailed off and the lush lips curved into a provocative smile. Was this what he had to look forward to if Nevil broke up with him? Men wanting nothing but a hookup? Damn.

"Thanks," he muttered and fled the room. He crossed the foyer to the front doors and stepped into the afternoon sunshine. Recovering his breath, he made his way to the train depot at the end of the block and caught the light rail home.

His mood plummeted further when he approached the brownstone and saw the empty driveway. Letting himself in, he sighed at the depressive silence as he closed the door behind him.

Shelton pushed off the smothering weight of loneliness. Nevil wasn't having everything his way. There was nothing to stop Shelton from catching a taxi and confronting him at the lake house. So what if he was going to Denver? There wasn't anything to keep him from coming home to Portland on weekends. Oregon was only a few hours away from Colorado by plane.

He pulled his cell phone from a pocket on the way to the kitchen for a snack to appease his rumbling stomach. He'd already pressed the number for the taxi service he frequented when a glittering item on the countertop caught his attention. He ended the call and set the phone on the table and his briefcase on the ground, his movements slow and careful as he took in what he saw.

The ring he'd given Nevil with such love six months ago sat on a slip of paper by the coffeepot. Nevil wasn't playing fair. Shelton knew he was hurt and disappointed, but did Nevil have to torture him like this? He went to the counter and swore, frustrated. The note claimed Nevil was too angry to talk with him. That he'd call later in the week. But that Shelton should have the ring back if he was determined to leave.

Shelton picked up the ring, his heart sore. "I'm sorry, Nevil." He mourned and kissed the cool trinket, wishing with all his heart he had Nevil's lips to kiss.

His heart jumped at a light rap on the door. Sometimes Nevil forgot his key. Shelton hurried to the foyer and took a habitual glance through the peephole. He frowned. "Andrew?" he asked as he opened the door. "Can I help you?" Shelton felt the heat rise in his face when Andrew lifted a brow.

"May I come in? Just for a moment," Andrew clarified when Shelton hesitated.

"This really isn't a good time." Shelton widened his eyes in surprise when Andrew shouldered past him as he started to close the door. He still held Nevil's ring and slipped it into his pocket. Andrew glanced into the empty rooms and then turned to Shelton.

"You seem to be alone," he said, and his gaze raked Shelton from head to toe.

Shelton grimaced, feeling like he'd just been undressed. "For the moment. What do you want that you couldn't tell me at the office?"

Andrew moved closer to him, and Shelton drew a sharp breath at the naked desire in his dark eyes. Andrew stood several inches taller than him, and Shelton had to fight the urge to step back.

"You should leave," he managed to say before Andrew's full lips descended on his. He wrenched his mouth free and fumbled for the door handle behind him.

Andrew put an arm on either side of him, holding the door closed. "Come on. What's the problem? You know I've wanted you. And since you're leaving anyway, where's the harm in a little fun?"

Before Shelton could answer, Andrew dropped his hand to the small of Shelton's back and pulled him closer. *This is ridiculous!* He wasn't the fainting heroine of some romance novel. A well-placed knee would put an end to his obvious interest, but what then? Shelton had never been in a fight in his life. How embarrassing to have to explain to Nevil if things got broken. Especially if it was him.

The thought made Shelton angry. "Andrew, you have one minute to leave before I call the police."

Andrew looked down at him, his smile mocking. "And tell them what? You let me in, remember? Besides, do you really want to explain to them what I'm doing here? I don't suppose they'd be sympathetic." He ground a fascinatingly large erection against Shelton's hip as he whispered in Shelton's ear, "You got the job in Denver over me. The least you could do is let me suck on you. Your cock has to be as beautiful as the rest of you."

Shelton's temper flared. "Don't be a fool. Just because Nevil and I are having a fight doesn't mean I'll play around with you. Now get the hell out."

"And if I don't?"

"Then I tell the police you raped me. They'll listen to that."

Anger swept over the handsome face. Andrew grabbed the back of Shelton's head and gave him a bruising kiss, his tongue plunging deep, choking him. He then let him go with a sneer. "Your loss, babe. Have a nice life."

Shelton stared at the door after Andrew left. Did he really just say that? What an ass. He ran a hand over his curls, at once exhausted from a sleepless night and a roller coaster of emotions. Sighing, he went into the living room and lay prone on the couch, unhappy and lonely. His estranged parents lived on the east coast with his younger brother, who never answered his calls, and now he was losing Nevil. What was he to do? He settled into the cushions, closing his tired eyes. As he drifted off, he heard the poignant tones of a favorite song playing in the distance.

He jerked awake and scrambled from the couch, rushing to get his phone. It fell silent and then played the wonderful notes of a message received. Nevil! His hand shook as he pressed the Playback button. A slow grin spread across his face as he listened.

"Sorry you didn't pick up. I miss your voice. Um... Sorry for leaving my ring like that. What a flaming drama queen. I was angry. Anyway, as you know, Barker has a cousin who's also in construction. A minor emergency has come up with his company, and I'm flying out to see if I can help. I'll try to be back before you leave. If not, be safe. But I'll try to be there. Anyway, wanted to let you know I'm sorry. Love you. Call you soon."

Shelton laughed, sleepy and happy. He and Nevil still needed to talk, but the world was right again. He went to the bedroom, his heart light, and stripped before climbing under the covers to finish his nap. He fell asleep on Nevil's pillow with the phone pressed to his ear, listening to Nevil's voice repeat its loving message.

*

Shelton woke a few hours later, still drowsy. He tried to catch the tendril of the erotic dream he'd been enjoying, but it faded with disappointing quickness, as did the sensation of Nevil's lips sliding over his dick. Still painfully aroused, Shelton rolled to his side and opened the drawer on the nightstand. He smiled in delighted anticipation. Nevil had returned the silk scarves and toy he'd used on Shelton at the lake, squeaky clean.

Nevil's own vibrator had been pushed to the back of the drawer, and Shelton ran his fingers over it, remembering Nevil's shuddering pleasure the few times Shelton had slid it into his ass. It was larger than the one Nevil had bought for him, and he frowned, wondering if there were men that big. He remembered being held against Andrew Blake's body. His pole had pushed hard into his hip. It might have been that large...

Shelton scowled and tossed the unwanted vibrator to the back of the drawer, then grabbed the lubricant and his own toy. After wiggling under the covers, he lay on his side and squeezed the jelly onto the end of the vibrator. He stroked himself, wishing Nevil was there to play with him.

He thought of Nevil's mouth on the tip of his cock, sucking him, the skillful tongue sliding over the slit and driving him crazy with pleasure. He pressed the vibrator against his hole and nudged it inside, grunting into the pillow before it slipped past the initial resistance and went in deep. He slid it in and out of his trembling body with slow strokes, imagining Nevil's fantastic dick inside him.

When his arm tired, Shelton found the right spot with the vibrator's bent tip and turned it on. He moaned as tingling pleasure spread through his body. Settling into the mattress, he stroked his erection, the slippery lubricant on his hand heating with the friction.

He kept the vibrator on its lowest setting, letting the orgasm build slowly. In his mind, he kissed Nevil and ran his tongue down his silky skin, pausing a moment to lick the hard buds on his sculpted chest before continuing lower. His orgasm came in a shattering surge of pleasure as he imagined taking Nevil's hard length into his mouth.

Chapter Four

Shelton sighed and rubbed his tired face. The weekend had seemed endless, and Monday and Tuesday were spent in long meetings and even longer evenings at home. At least the usual Wednesday staff meeting had been brief. It gave him time after lunch to phone his clients and set up an initial interview for them with Andrew Blake, who was taking over his portfolio when he left.

There was a knock on the open door of his office, and he glanced up, but his smile turned sour. Speak of the devil.

"Do you have that list yet?" Andrew asked as he came into the room. Instead of walking up to the desk as expected, he turned and closed the door. Shelton put his pen down and sat up straighter. What was he up to?

Andrew sauntered over and sat on the edge of Shelton's desk. "Now we won't be disturbed."

"Here are the names of my clients and the times they can see you." Shelton slid the notepaper across the desk. Andrew picked it up and read through it.

"Who's this?"

Shelton leaned toward him to read the name, and Andrew abruptly stood and rounded the desk. He leaned over Shelton's shoulder and underscored a name with a thick finger. "I can't make out these initials."

Shelton cleared his throat before answering, shifting in his chair. Andrew's subtle cologne teased his senses while the heat from where their bodies touched caused warmth to spread through him. Damn, the man was large. He shrugged his shoulder, trying to give Andrew the hint to back off. In answer, Andrew pushed his cock harder into Shelton's side.

"Well?"

Shelton looked up at him, and Andrew seized his lips in a brutal kiss, grabbing the back of his head so he couldn't pull away. Shelton felt blindly for the edge of the desk and pushed his chair out, then scrambled to his feet.

"Are you out of your mind?" he asked on a ragged breath and wiped his mouth with the back of a shaking hand.

"Come on. Don't play coy." Andrew took a step toward him.

Shelton held his ground as Andrew came right up to him and stopped just shy of touching him.

"I gave you my answer the other night, Andrew."

"But there's been several lonely nights in between, haven't there?"

Shelton stared at him, and Andrew explained. "I've heard the rumors. Nevil doesn't come home anymore. Is he sleeping with someone else?" He put a hand on Shelton's chest, over his wildly beating heart. "Does that hurt? I can help you with it."

Jesus Christ. Why had he ever told Ted Pringle that Nevil was gone a few days? Should have known the guy would dramatize it. "Andrew, just get the hell out of my office. Try this again and I'll make a complaint of sexual harassment."

Andrew drew himself to his full height, but Shelton didn't budge at the implied threat. He wouldn't be bullied. He felt uneasy, though, at Andrew's next words. "You're not uptight. There's too much passion in your eyes. You must still be horning after that prick of a boyfriend." He tapped his lips with a finger. "But if he were out of the picture…"

Andrew swiveled and strode across the room, leaving the door open as he left. Shelton watched him go, feeling numb. What had Andrew meant? Scarier still, what was the fucker going to do? He raced after Andrew and collided with Ted Pringle, who hovered in the doorway.

"Sorry," he muttered, grabbing Ted's arm to steady him.

Ted gave him a wide smile. "Don't worry about it. You can bump into me anytime." His expression turned shrewd. "Was that Andrew coming out of your office? Seemed in a hurry. What's going on with you two?"

Shelton studied Ted's guileless blue eyes. Ted was a ferocious gossip, but maybe that was what he needed. If Andrew's play at intimidating him spread through the office, he might back off. He pulled Ted against the wall and whispered, "Can you keep a secret?"

*

Shelton took his time walking home from the light rail train stop. The sun felt good on his face and warmed his chilled bones. He hadn't seen Andrew again the rest of the afternoon, for which he was thoroughly glad. Andrew's hint of somehow getting rid of Nevil had unnerved him. He needed to plan what he should do about it, if anything. Shelton didn't believe Andrew would hurt Nevil physically, but lies could sometimes be more damaging.

He snorted in disgust. It wasn't as if Andrew loved him. He was one of those guys who wanted something simply because it was out of their reach. Andrew seemed driven to succeed at work. Shelton hoped he didn't apply that same singlemindedness to pursuing him. Shit.

Concentrating on his problems, Shelton jumped when his phone buzzed. He smiled when he read who was calling.

"Hi, Tera."

"Can you come to the studio tonight?"

"Um...sure." Shelton laughed fondly at Tera's rushed words.

"Sorry to be so abrupt. I need to retake several of the pictures we did last week, and I'm really pressed for time."

"It's no problem. Nevil's out of town anyway."

"What's my brother up to this time?"

Shelton gave a slight shrug, recalling Nevil's cryptic message. "He said he would be helping out his boss's cousin, but you know how he is about calling. I haven't heard from him since he left on Friday."

"Typical. How do you put up with him?"

A pang of regret stole Shelton's breath for a second. Nothing had been settled between them. He would put up with Nevil forever if he gave Shelton the chance. There had to be a way to make it work out.

"Shelton, everything okay?"

"We'll talk tonight. I'm walking home at the moment."

"Sure. And Shelton, you know Nevil loves you no matter how much of an ass he might be at times."

"I know that, dear. See you tonight."

Shelton slipped the phone back into his pocket, wondering how many pictures he'd need to redo for Nevil's twin. He was glad it was the charcoal-gray suit. Nevil had admired him in it, and Shelton enjoyed trying on the exclusive suits and jackets Tera designed.

He glanced up from the sidewalk as he turned the corner of his street. Nevil! The Prius sat in the driveway of the brownstone. Heart hammering, he hurried to the front door, then hesitated, chewing his lip as he removed the chain holding Nevil's ring from around his neck.

He was still looking at it doubtfully when the door flung open. Strong hands reached for him and pulled him into Nevil's crushing embrace.

"Nevil—"

He gave up trying to speak as Nevil kissed him over and over, making little sounds of delight. Shelton had the presence of mind to nudge the door closed with a foot, and then he slipped his tongue into the sweet heat of Nevil's mouth, savoring the taste of him. His body caught fire under Nevil's wandering hands.

"I've missed you," Nevil confessed and ground his hips against Shelton's, showing him just how much. Shelton's body grew just as hard and yearning, and he pushed against Nevil, urging him toward the living room.

Nevil drew him along and then paused at a soft clink on the floor.

He bent down and picked up the chain. "What's this?" he said, sounding puzzled.

Shelton's heart dropped to his feet. He didn't want to talk about it right then. He wanted to take Nevil to the couch, strip, and climb onto his lap. He took a steadying breath. It was probably better to get it over with.

"I was hoping you'd take it back. It doesn't mean..." Damn, it was hard to say with Nevil looking so eager. He tore his gaze away from his face and stared at the tiles under his feet. "I don't expect you to spend your nights alone when I'm gone, but I was hoping you'd want to see me on weekends."

Nevil touched his chin, raising his face. Shelton blinked in surprise. Nevil's lovely turquoise eyes sparkled with unexpected laughter. A soft smile played on the corners of his lips. "My sweet Shelton. No wonder I'm so crazy in love with you."

Shelton's gasp drowned in a torrid kiss. Nevil nibbled his lips and sucked his tongue, and Shelton's body ached with longing for his sure touch, his mind whirling from the erotic play.

"Please," he murmured, not sure if he begged Nevil to end the sweet torture or to continue forever. Nevil's answer was to slip his hand into Shelton's pants and grip his cock. Shelton moaned into Nevil's mouth, fighting for breath while Nevil kissed, stroked, and squeezed him. Shelton became lightheaded with intense pleasure and lack of air, and it took a minute to recall what he wanted to do.

"Wait." He put a little space between their heated bodies and grabbed Nevil's wrist as Nevil continued to fondle him. He had five days of loneliness to make up for and wanted this to last. "I want to go first."

Nevil grinned, and a wicked light sprang into his eyes. "Anything you say." He gave Shelton's hard dick one last promising squeeze, then stepped back from him.

Shelton's gaze traveled over Nevil, and he trembled in anticipation of loving that gorgeous body. "Take off your shirt," he commanded and smiled to hear Nevil's delighted laugh at his stern tone. Nevil went to the couch, put the chain holding his ring on the coffee table, and then lifted his shirt. Shelton lost his breath in a surge of pure lust as Nevil pulled it over his head. Nevil ran every morning, and his sculpted chest was golden from the sun. Neither he nor Shelton had much hair, but a smattering of dark curls started at Nevil's navel and flowed in a tantalizing line downward, ending in a silken nest that always teased and tickled Shelton's skin.

Shelton wanted to lick his way down the dark line and bury his face in the heated tangle of curls, rich with Nevil's heady scent. He wanted to press kisses on the delicious cock nestled there before taking it into his mouth.

"Undo your pants. I want to see you."

Nevil chuckled. "Someone's being naughty."

Heat flushed through Shelton at the glee in Nevil's voice, and he watched, captivated, as Nevil undid the button and zipper of his pants. He nudged them down his hips, slowly revealing the black briefs beneath with its definite bulge. Shelton moistened his lips, then grabbed Nevil's wrist, stopping him from lowering the clothing further.

Obediently, Nevil put his hands behind his back.

Shelton stroked Nevil's erection through the soft fabric of the briefs and then slid the waistband down to reveal the glistening tip. He was unable to resist the temptation and knelt to lick at the precome, loving the tang of it on his tongue. He stood and kissed Nevil's dark nipples, careful not to touch him in any other way. He grazed one hardening bud with his teeth, shivering pleasantly at the moan it drew from Nevil. He looked up into his turquoise eyes and kissed his parted mouth, savoring its sweetness.

He drew back and relished the flush of passion on Nevil's face and the gleam in his eyes, tracing the full bottom lip with his thumb. Nevil nipped at him, and Shelton flamed to life at the pain, his erection hard and straining against his zipper.

"Take them off and kneel on the couch, facing the wall," Shelton said, voice rough with desire.

"As you wish," Nevil said with a slight bow and stripped off his pants and briefs. He climbed onto the couch, legs spread, presenting his tight ass. Shelton moved behind him, ran a finger down his crack, and teased his hole before slipping his hand under to hold the heavy balls.

He gave a thought to changing his mind, wanting to have Nevil's beautiful cock thrusting inside him. He was rarely the man on top, preferring to have Nevil buried deep inside him when he came. He'd been lonely, though. He wanted the added closeness, that feeling of being one with Nevil, this time.

He patted the pretty butt and nibbled on Nevil's ear. "I'll be right back."

"Hurry."

Shelton trotted to their room and retrieved the bottle of lube and a towel from the bathroom. He stopped in the archway to the living room on the way back and drank in the sight of Nevil's tanned and lithe muscled body kneeling on the couch. His head tilted toward the framed Monet print on the wall just in front of him as he absently fondled himself. Shelton grinned, his body tingling with excitement as he returned to Nevil and handed him the towel.

"What, no toys?"

Shelton paused with his scarred cock in his hand. He thrust off his doubts. Nevil had never made him feel unwanted. He leaned on Nevil's sleek back and worked lubed fingers into him.

"Only me today, dear," he said and pressed the tip of his erection against Nevil's puckered hole.

"Fantastic," Nevil said, and his deep groan of pleasure as Shelton pushed into him dissolved Shelton's lingering insecurities. He'd wanted to tease a little and quickly pull out, but Nevil pushed back against him, driving Shelton deeper into the tight heat of his body.

"You like that?" Shelton whispered between breaths, desperate not to come too quickly as pleasure radiated through him.

Nevil gripped the back of the couch. "Harder," he demanded.

Shelton slid his hands down Nevil's tense, sweaty back and then slipped a hand around to rub his hard balls. He trailed a finger along Nevil's tight shaft.

Nevil whimpered. "Shelton."

Shelton's restraint broke at the pleading note. He gripped Nevil's hips and thrust deep. Spurred on by Nevil's shout, he plunged again into the yielding body, and Nevil met him with equal enthusiasm.

At last, unable to hold back the ecstasy boiling in his sac, Shelton reached around and stroked Nevil's rock-hard cock in time with his thrusts.

Nevil's cry rang in the room. "Now!"

He jerked in Shelton's hand, and Shelton came. He lost track of Nevil, the world narrowing to the pleasure surging from his cock into Nevil's body.

It took a moment to come back to himself, aware of his arms wrapped around Nevil's waist, his cheek pressed to Nevil's warm back. He tasted sweat on his lips, and he inhaled the tantalizing scent of their lovemaking.

Tears scalded his eyes. He didn't want to leave. How would he bear being away from this man who embodied everything to him? He listened to Nevil's heartbeat slow under his ear and eased out of him.

Nevil glanced over his shoulder, and his lovely eyes widened. He quickly wadded up the towel and tossed it on the floor and then pulled Shelton into his arms on the couch, petted and kissed him. His gentleness eased the pain in Shelton's chest.

"Better?"

Shelton nodded and wiped at his eyes. Nevil caught his hand and kissed the tears one by one from his face with soft, butterfly kisses. He nuzzled Shelton's ear. "What's wrong?"

Shelton drew a deep breath. "I'm the biggest fool, Nevil. Will you see me on weekends if I come home?"

"You won't have to come back that often. I—"

Shelton's heart gave a painful thump, but he told it to be still. "If that's what you want…" he said over Nevil's words, not wanting to hear the reasons.

Nevil cupped his chin and made him look into his eyes. "I'm coming with you."

Shelton blinked, afraid of the joy that sprang inside him. What if he'd misunderstood? "What?"

"I'm going with you. There's no way in hell I'm going to risk losing you to some gorgeous ski bunny in Colorado." He pulled Shelton against his shoulder and absently played with his curls. "I went straight to Mr. Barker after leaving here Friday, told him I needed to speak with his cousin about a job. Randal's company has branched out to most of the Midwest states, and they have an office in Denver. I flew out to meet with him, and he offered me the job as their architectural design consultant."

Shelton laced his fingers with Nevil's and brought their hands to his lips, his throat too tight to speak.

"It's only for one week a month, and then I spend the other three here. And I don't know how long this job in Denver will last," Nevil cautioned.

"Nevil, I'll do everything possible to make this work. I know you want to stay here. If things get too complicated, I'll quit. I'd rather serve coffee in some bistro than lose you."

Nevil held him close. "Deal," he said and kissed Shelton's trembling lips. Shelton swore when his phone rang, this time playing the song he'd chosen for Tera.

"My sister's timing is as bad as ever," Nevil grumbled, sitting up.

"I forgot. I'm supposed to meet her at the studio to retake some pictures."

"You'd better go, then. She owes me for this, though. I'll give you a ride and pick up dinner."

"Spicy would be nice," Shelton suggested. He dialed Tera's number as he followed Nevil to the bedroom for a shower.

Chapter Five

Nevil drove Shelton to Tera's studio downtown but put a hand on Shelton's knee before he could leave the car. "I'll pick up Thai food around the corner and be right back."

Shelton looked at him, curious what he was thinking, when Nevil continued to hold him in place. Nevil leaned across the seat and kissed him. "What are you modeling?"

"The gray suit. Tera didn't like the lighting on it."

Nevil's gaze traveled over him and then back up to meet his eyes. "Delicious."

Shelton's face heated at the open admiration. "I love you. See you in a minute," he told Nevil and climbed from the car. He took a breath of cool evening air as Nevil drove off. A smattering of stars twinkled overhead, and feeling whimsical, he made a wish on one of them. He failed to see the hooded figure that stepped out of the alley until it was too late to call Nevil back.

"Hi, Shelton."

Shelton eyed the man, wary. "Andrew," he said, his heart pounding. A current of fear stole his breath when he saw Andrew's clenched hands. Andrew was a large man and could probably kick his ass. He wondered if he could talk his way out of this.

Andrew jerked his head. "In the alley."

"But…"

He winced when Andrew grabbed his arm. "You made me look like a fool at the bank. Now, we can talk back there, or I can simply punch you in the throat."

Shelton's pulse jumped, acutely aware of their seclusion on the street, quiet at that time of night. Without waiting for an answer, Andrew dragged him into the shadows between the buildings and shoved him into a brick wall, jarring his back.

Andrew pressed the length of his body against him. Shelton could smell tequila on his breath. He'd probably been at the bar up the street and ducked into the alley to relieve himself. Shelton wrinkled his nose at the thought.

Andrew nipped Shelton's earlobe. "I see the boyfriend's back in the picture. Did you fuck him?"

Shelton's mind raced. There had to be a way out of this dreadful situation. The mad gleam in Andrew's eyes frightened him. He turned his face when Andrew tried to kiss him and shuddered as he licked Shelton's cheek. Andrew kissed him, biting Shelton's lip, and Shelton tasted blood mixed with the alcohol on his tongue. Andrew slid his free hand down Shelton's body and gripped him through his pants. Shelton shuddered again and wondered how far he'd get if he kneed Andrew in the groin and ran for the street.

Andrew dropped his head, sucked on Shelton's neck, and bit none too gently. "You've snubbed me for years. There's nothing to stop me from taking your ass right here and now."

"Except me."

They both looked up in surprise at the intrusion, and Shelton lurched back as Nevil swung his arm, the brick in his hand connecting with the side of Andrew's head. He dropped to a knee with a guttural cry of pain. Andrew clutched at the gash on his forehead and then staggered to his feet, fury mottling the part of his face not covered with dripping blood. Nevil faced him coolly, hefting the brick in his palm.

Shelton gave a nervous laugh. The whole situation was intolerable. "Andrew," he said, pulling his phone from a pocket and showing it to him. "You have three seconds to leave before I call the police."

Andrew's gaze darted between the two of them. "This isn't over, Shelton," he swore, though there was a note of uncertainty in his voice.

Damn it. Shelton refused to feel sorry for him, even if he did seem drunk off his ass. But there was no excuse for what he'd tried to do.

Nevil stepped between them. "It is over, asshole. If you come anywhere near Shelton again, I swear to God I'll make you sorry for it."

Shelton shivered a little at the cold certainty in Nevil's voice. Andrew seemed to believe it too. With a last desperate look at Shelton, he jogged down the alley and disappeared around the corner of the building. Shelton watched him go and hugged his arms to his chest as his body shook. He was grateful when Nevil pulled him close, warming him.

Nevil searched Shelton's face and cursed under his breath. "Let's get you inside and take a look at that cut lip," he said with stifled anger.

Shelton met his eyes. "I'm fine, Nevil. Really. Though I'm very glad you came when you did."

"I was coming back to see what kind of sauce you wanted with dinner when Andrew dragged you in here. God, I've never been so furious in my life."

"Never mind. It's over. Let's see if Tera will make us a cup of tea. I'm not hungry anymore."

"All right." Nevil took his arm protectively as they walked to the studio. Shelton braced himself as they rang the bell. Sure enough, Tera took one look at him and pulled him into the studio, asking a million questions as she led him to the small kitchen area in the back. The room contained a microwave, a small refrigerator, and a sink, plus a table and two chairs. Shelton and Nevil took the chairs while Tera wet a soft cloth and pressed it to Shelton's still bleeding lip.

"Really, I'm fine," Shelton reiterated after Nevil told the story of what had happened.

Nevil pushed back his chair and paced the small area. "I could kill that bastard."

"Did you call the police?" Tera asked. Shelton shook his head. Tera was as beautiful as her twin and just as angry, but if they didn't change the subject, he was going to scream.

"Can we drop it? It's over, and I'd rather forget it ever happened. If Andrew tries anything more, I promise I'll report him."

Nevil gave him a tight smile. "Sorry, darling. I want to find Andrew and beat the life out of him."

Shelton let out an exasperated breath, and Tera patted his hand. "It's okay. We're just concerned for you. What a horrible experience."

"Can I change now?" Shelton asked, growing impatient. "I'd like to get the pictures done and go home."

"Oh, of course." Tera sent her brother an uncertain look. "The suit is in the closet there. I'll set up the lighting."

Shelton watched Nevil pace after Tera had left the room and felt the first, delicious stirrings of passion. He'd never seen Nevil do anything more violent than kill a spider in the bathtub. He squirmed on the chair, a little embarrassed to find Nevil's aggression on his behalf aroused him.

"Nevil," he called in a soft tone.

Nevil stopped, looked at him, and quickly came to his side. "What is it?"

Shelton remained seated, gazing up into the beautiful eyes full of concern. A smile spread on his face. "My hero," he drawled. "I think I have a fangirl crush on you."

Nevil blinked several times, and then a dark flush rose in his face. He pulled Shelton up into his arms. "I'm sorry this happened," he murmured and put a soft kiss on the bruises peppering Shelton's neck.

"Me too." Shelton gave him a fierce hug and then took a step back, turning his face to the light. "How does it look?"

"It's only a nick and not bleeding anymore, though your lip's a little puffy. Goddammit. What about the pictures?"

"Tera can photograph my left profile. It's my best side, anyway."

"If you say so. You'd better dress," Nevil said as Tera called from the other room.

"Only if you help me."

"Of course." Nevil closed the kitchen door.

*

Shelton lay awake that night in the cool darkness of the bedroom, illuminated by the faint glow of the digital clock. What a terrible day. At least they'd be traveling on the weekend, and he could put it all behind him.

"Are you awake?"

Shelton groped for Nevil's hand. There'd been a note of anxiousness in the beloved voice that touched his heart.

"What's wrong, sweetheart?"

"I don't know. I can't seem to catch my breath."

Shelton rolled to his side and put a hand on Nevil's chest. Sure enough, his heart raced under his palm. He could hear Nevil's panting in the semidarkness, though he could barely make out Nevil's features. The skin proved hot when he placed the back of his hand against his cheek.

"Do you feel sick?"

Nevil sighed. "No, but it feels like my heart keeps skipping a beat. Do you think I might be having a stroke?"

Shelton hugged Nevil close. He knew what this was. Nevil stood strong in so many other ways, but there were times when his own body frightened him.

"Would you feel better if we checked your symptoms online?"

Nevil let out a worried breath. "Would you mind? I'm sorry. I just feel..."

Shelton found Nevil's mouth with his and gave him a gentle kiss. "I don't mind at all. You know that. Come on."

He took Nevil by the hand, climbed out of bed, and then padded on bare feet into the hallway. Nevil snatched up their bathrobes on the way out and put one around Shelton's shoulders as he opened the laptop on the desk in the living room.

Nevil pulled up a chair next to him, and Shelton squeezed his knee. "What are your complaints again?"

Shelton scrolled through the charts referring to Nevil's symptoms, finding the answer after several minutes of searching.

Nevil sputtered at the result. "Anxiety? You mean my chest feels like it's going to seize up because I'm anxious?"

"It's been a hard week, ending with that frightening scene in the alley." Shelton cupped Nevil's scowling face. "This is my fault. I'm sorry."

Nevil looked away from him, but Shelton saw the red in his cheeks. He put his arms loosely around Nevil's shoulders. "Don't be embarrassed. I'm glad you found out what's wrong rather than wait until you made yourself sick with worry. Do you want to stay up and talk for a while?"

Nevil shrugged, and Shelton rose to his feet and tugged on his robe. "Come to bed. Let me hold you. We can talk or not, and you can have a good run in the morning. That usually helps you feel better." He turned off the computer and put an arm around Nevil's waist, drawing him to the bedroom and into his arms under the covers.

"Try to sleep," he murmured and tucked his head into Nevil's shoulder. Nevil held him tight but didn't speak, and Shelton was content to simply be there for him. He listened to Nevil's heartbeat until it slowed and his breathing grew even. Then Shelton rolled to his back and stared at the darkness over the bed.

He should never have scared Nevil like that, making plans without discussing them first. Fortunately, this episode had been a mild one. Nevil's anxiety attack last winter had been very real, sending him to the hospital with the fear that he was dying or losing his mind—or both.

Shelton had to be more careful with him.

Nevil stirred on the bed beside him. "Are you awake?"

Shelton grinned at the ceiling somewhere in the dark over his head. He knew that tone, and his body tingled in anticipation of the pleasures that usually followed when Nevil used it.

"Maybe," he drawled, purposefully coy, giving Nevil the challenge he relished. Nevil moved closer and rested on an elbow. "You're so good to me." Nevil's fingers strayed to his chest and tweaked a nipple, and Shelton shivered with pleasure.

"Aren't you supposed to be sleeping?" he teased, losing his breath when Nevil flicked his tongue over the hardening bud on his chest. Nevil chuckled, reached for him, and captured Shelton's lips with a kiss while he slid his hand across Shelton's hip to cup his balls. Shelton stretched languidly, loving the feel of Nevil's sleek body against him as he lay wrapped in Nevil's arms.

Nevil deepened their kiss, and Shelton ran his fingers through the thick hair, smiling with fondness. Nevil hated to have his hair messed with at any other time, but now he purred like a contented kitten. Nevil burrowed into his neck, and Shelton pushed him off with a laugh.

"None of that! It tickles."

"Too bad," Nevil countered, trying for Shelton's neck again. Shelton wrestled with him and then lay back against the pillows and opened his arms.

"Fine. Do whatever you like."

"Damn straight," Nevil murmured and kissed the pulse beating rapidly in Shelton's neck. The dark head lowered, and a pleasant shiver ran through Shelton. The talented fingers and amazing tongue traveled the muscles of his shoulders and chest, pausing a second to nip gently at a vulnerable nipple before moving downward.

Nevil stopped at Shelton's hipbone. Shelton trembled, his pulse rioting as the seconds ticked by and Nevil made no move. He startled when a finger brushed over his lips in the dark. Knowing what Nevil wanted, he drew the digit into his mouth, getting it as wet as he could. He shivered with anticipation when Nevil trailed his hand down Shelton's body, over his balls, and moaned when the wet finger nudged inside him.

His dick ached for attention. He felt Nevil's breath and cried out when Nevil circled the sensitive tip of his erection with his tongue then dipped into the slit. Nevil pushed another finger inside him and swallowed his dick at the same time, driving Shelton crazy with pleasure. Nevil's fingers did amazing things while the skilled mouth licked and sucked him, sending him to the edge of orgasm.

"Nevil—" He gasped in warning. Nevil gave a wicked chuckle around his cock and kept at it. Crying out in pleasure and love, Shelton came in Nevil's mouth, soaring into ecstasy. He sighed with bliss as he floated back into his body and his life with Nevil, his heart swelling with thankfulness for the wonderful future they still had together.

SHELTON'S

HOMECOMING

Chapter One

Shelton slowed to a walk as he approached the glass doors of the emergency ward. He could see nurses and doctors bustling around on the other side of the barrier.

Would they let him see Nevil?

"Shelton!"

He jumped on hearing his name and looked over his shoulder. Tera waved from further down the hall, and he waited for her, heart racing as Nevil's twin came up to him. He blinked at her brilliant smile and had trouble speaking past the lump in his throat. "What...?"

"He's not in there. He's doing so well they moved him to a regular room about an hour ago."

They grinned at each other in celebration. Shelton switched his overnight bag to his left hand and linked arms with Tera. He'd come straight from the airport, impatient to see the love of his life. "Take me to him."

"This way."

Tera led him back down the long hallway to the elevators, and Shelton cleared his throat as the doors closed behind them. "I'm glad you came when you did. I wasn't sure they'd let me see him in emergency care. I'm not immediate family."

"You could say you're married…"

He found a spot to look at on the floor. "Nevil would have a lot to say about that." Tera made a small sound of protest, and Shelton flashed a smile. "It's okay. So, Nevil's doing well?"

"He is. He's been sleeping a lot, but the doctor says he should recover without any trouble."

"Thank God." Shelton drew a deep breath. Relief washed through him in a wave that left him weak. Gathering his courage as the elevator came to a halt, he once again followed Tera down an endless hallway. He paused outside the open door to Nevil's room and then stepped inside, his gaze going at once to the precious man in the hospital bed.

Nevil looked so pale! His dark hair and bruised eyes were a stark contrast to the pristine sheets and pillow. All at once, Tera's frantic late afternoon call, the mad rush to the airport, and the crazy taxi drive to the hospital took their toll. Shelton brushed a shaky hand over his stinging eyes. *I won't cry, damn it!*

He approached the bed and gently put his hand on Nevil's shoulder, needing to touch him, and drank in the sight of his beautiful lover. Shelton willed Nevil to wake up and prove he was okay. He'd been terrified on the plane that he'd arrive too late and Nevil would be dead. Tera's call had been close to incoherent; he'd imagined the blackest scenarios.

Tera came up beside him and gave him an apologetic look. "There's a large lump on the back of his head. The whole thing was an accident, honey. Nevil stepped on some rotten floorboards in a building they're renovating and fell to the floor beneath. Maybe I shouldn't have called you until I knew how bad he was, but he was unconscious when they admitted him..."

"It's okay. I want to be here. I planned to come home this weekend anyway and only had to take a couple of personal days. It's fine."

He returned his gaze to Nevil's beloved face and tentatively caressed a bruised cheek, wanting him to wake up. He loved him so much. Remembering what Tera had said earlier about marriage, warmth spread through him. Husband? Sure, he could do that. He knew Nevil would smack him if he ever had the balls to call him wife, and his lips twitched with humor.

He took a deep breath. The point was moot anyway. They'd been to weddings of various friends, but Nevil had never shown the slightest interest in it for himself. Shelton smoothed the lines of pain from Nevil's forehead with a gentle finger. He knew Nevil remained devoted to him, and he would have to be content with that.

Nevil's dark lashes fluttered, and Shelton's heart stumbled. A gleam of turquoise flashed at him, and the tears he'd held off scalded his eyes. "Nevil?" he asked.

Nevil's gaze stayed blank, but then awareness swept in, and he said in a weak voice, "Shelton? God! I must be dying if you're here."

Shelton choked on a painful laugh. "Falling down on the job, honey?" he joked. Emotions tangled inside him, the strongest the desire to feel Nevil's sweet lips under his own. He wanted to climb onto the bed and pull Nevil close, never let him go. He'd been so damned scared.

As Nevil watched Shelton, his expression softened, and he reached out a hand to him. "Come here, love," he said fondly. Shelton sighed and sat on the edge of the bed and rested his head on Nevil's chest. He listened to the strong heartbeat under his ear and let the tears trickle down his face while Nevil stroked his hair. Relief unmanned him. What if Nevil had been seriously hurt or had died like he'd imagined?

"Shelton," Nevil whispered his name.

Shelton lifted his head and met Nevil's wonderful eyes, which brimmed with love and exhaustion.

"Shit, I'm sorry." He sat up and rubbed at his eyes. "Here I'm blubbering like a baby when you should be sleeping."

"I am tired. They've pumped me full of painkillers, but I won't sleep unless you kiss me goodnight."

Shelton felt the warmth in his cheeks as he blushed with pleasure. Idiot! Nevil was fine, wasn't he? He gave a hasty look over Nevil's form under the sheets. "You're not hurt anywhere else?"

Sleepy, Nevil chuckled. "Want to search me? I'm perfectly fine, love. The doctor says I'll have this headache for a few days, but he sees no reason why I shouldn't recover fully. The rest is just bruises and achy bones from the fall."

"You're lucky it wasn't your neck," Tera stated from the window where she tactfully waited. She came across to the bed and kissed Nevil's cheek. "Goodnight, dear. Shelton, I'll be in the hall when you're ready."

"I think I'll stay here tonight, but thanks."

Nevil's expression turned stubborn. "You will not, Shelton! I'm fine. Go home; you're done in."

"But..."

"I think there are enough people here to help me if I need it. Go on, sweetheart. I promise I'll be okay. Besides, I'd feel weird knowing you were watching me while I slept."

Shelton grimaced. He'd said that after one of their first nights together when he'd woken up to find Nevil staring at him. For a moment, he'd felt self-conscious but then and there changed his mind. One of his greatest delights became seeing Nevil propped up on his elbow in bed watching him in the morning. Nevil's lips would form a provocative curl, and Shelton's body would react instantly, springing to attention.

Nevil gave him a lewd wink, and Shelton shook his head and said, "You're such an ass. Good thing I love you so much or I might be tempted to leave you here for a week."

"Doctor Franklyn *is* rather cute..."

"That's not—"

"Shelton, shut up and kiss me already."

"If I have to," Shelton teased and settled more comfortably on the bed. He cupped Nevil's face, careful of the painful bruises, and leaned close to lick his top lip and gently suck on the fuller, soft bottom one. His pulse surged, cock responding to the memory of those delicious lips as they surrounded him and drew him into the heated depths of his mouth. He groaned and pushed his tongue between the sweet barrier where Nevil's tongue greeted him with delighted familiarity. Shelton deepened the contact; he wanted to climb into that honeyed warmth and lie safe in Nevil's embrace.

All at once, he felt embarrassed and pulled back. Nevil lay injured and in pain, and here he attempted to indulge his own needs.

"I'm sorry. I guess I've missed you," he mumbled, trying to slow his heartbeat.

Nevil gave him a sleepy smile and licked his lips. "I missed you too. Mmm... that was nice. Once I'm home..." His voice trailed off, and Shelton watched his eyes drift closed, face softening into sleep. A slight snore escaped Nevil's parted lips, and Shelton's heart swelled with love.

"Goodnight, sweetheart," he said, and he stole one more kiss to take with him. Shelton jerked upright when he heard a polite cough at the doorway.

The doctor watched him with amusement. "Am I interrupting?"

Heat warmed Shelton's face. "He's fallen asleep again."

The doctor crossed the room and held out his hand. "I'm Doctor Franklyn. Tera warned me you were in here."

Shelton shook his hand and then waited by the bed while he checked Nevil's vitals. Damn, the man *was* cute.

"How is he?" he asked when the doctor straightened from listening to Nevil's heart.

Franklyn gave him a kind smile. "I understand your concern, but he'll be fine. He hit the wall when he fell and might be concussed, which is why I want to keep him overnight. His hardhat saved him from anything worse. As it is, he'll have a headache for the next few days. He's also bruised his elbow pretty bad and has a fabulous bruise on his hip. I'll prescribe something for the pain, but there's no reason why he shouldn't be able to go home tomorrow."

Shelton couldn't stop the grin that spread on his face. "That's good to hear."

Chapter Two

Shelton sat in contemplative silence as Tera drove him to the brownstone he and Nevil shared, at least on the weekends he was home. Nevil's consulting job in Colorado had come to an end last month. Now Shelton's promotion at the bank seven months ago and consequential move to Colorado, everything he'd worked so hard to attain, seemed like the worst mistake of his life. He'd forced Nevil into the compromise of a long-distance relationship through his selfishness. He groaned into his hands. Without Nevil, he'd lived a half-life. The thought filled him with regret. He wouldn't do that anymore.

"Shelton, are you okay?"

Tera's concern touched him, and he smiled at her in the semi-darkness of the car. "Yeah. Tired and depressed, but nothing a good night's sleep won't cure."

"I'm sorry I scared you."

"Nonsense, I think you woke me up to what's wrong in my life."

Tera gave him a quick glance but let him alone when he didn't elaborate. In a few moments, they pulled into the driveway of the house, and Shelton let out a relieved breath. He was home.

"Thanks, Tera. I'll call you in the morning, okay?"

"I have a couple of errands to run, but I can swing by and give you a lift to the hospital."

"That's okay. I'll just catch the train in." He leaned over and kissed her cheek. "Goodnight."

"Goodnight." She put a hand on his arm as he made to leave. "I'm really glad you're here. I know Nevil is too. Thanks for coming."

Shelton gave her a nod and climbed from the car. He waved as she drove away, then faced the brownstone. A weight seemed to drop from his shoulders. He fished his keys from a pocket, let himself in, and flipped on a light. The familiar sights and smells filled his senses, and he smiled. Nevil's drafting supplies covered every available flat surface, and his own books and artwork filled the shelves. Their lives meshed. He didn't need marriage vows to tell him that.

Deciding to shower before anything else, he took his overnight bag to the bedroom. A smile curled his lips as he stared at the wide expanse of bed in the middle of the room. Nevil would be in that bed tomorrow. His heartbeat quickened, and he laughed a little as his cock stirred. He hadn't been with Nevil in over a week. It seemed like an eternity when he craved his touch every night.

Shelton closed his eyes and envisioned Nevil standing in front of him; he knew that decadent look on his face.

Nevil cupped his chin and brushed Shelton's lips with his own in an ardent kiss. His skillful fingers unbuttoned Shelton's shirt and undid the belt on his slacks...

Shelton blinked his eyes open and hurried to strip. His cock jutted skyward as he crossed the floor to the bathroom and turned on the faucets in the shower. Stepping under the spray, he sighed with bliss as the hot water struck his shoulders. He licked his lips and closed his eyes, eager to continue the fantasy he'd started in the bedroom...

Nevil climbed in the stall with him, his gorgeous turquoise eyes gleaming with love and lust. He took Shelton's mouth in a kiss that burned him to the core.

Nevil's fingers explored Shelton's body; they teased and tugged. He picked up the soap and rubbed it over Shelton's chest, his free hand tweaking Shelton's hard nipples, sending jolts of pleasure through him.

"Face the wall," Nevil whispered in his ear. *Yes!* Shelton obediently turned and planted his feet apart, shivering with anticipation as Nevil stepped behind him. He held his breath. Then Nevil touched the small of his back and traveled his finger down the crack of his ass to tease his hole. Shelton moaned with need. They kept lube beside the shampoo, and soon Nevil pushed his finger inside him. Shelton's muscles clenched around it at once, his legs shaking as Nevil massaged the tight ring. Another finger followed the first, and they worked in unison to prepare him.

Nevil reached around to knead his balls, and Shelton threw his head back on Nevil's shoulder, groaning aloud as Nevil's fingers continued to push in and out of his hole, driving him wild. The fingers withdrew, and Shelton braced for Nevil's thick, gorgeous cock taking their place and inching into his ass, filling him. Nevil shifted behind him, and Shelton cried out, Nevil's dick sliding over that perfect spot. Nevil gripped Shelton's slippery shaft and pumped him while his deep thrusts continued to stroke his prostate, sending Shelton over the edge. He came with a shout and burst of semen while Nevil continued to move inside him, drawing out his pleasure...

It took a moment for Shelton to catch his breath and come back to reality, and then he released his spent cock and pulled his fingers out of his hole. His body tingled wonderfully, but his fantasies were never as good as the real thing.

Fishing the soap off the floor, he washed his body and then rinsed the shower tiles. When done, he turned the water off and stepped onto the soft rug, reaching for a towel. As he dried off, he decided he wasn't very hungry and left the bathroom to climb at once into the empty bed. He pulled Nevil's pillow into his arms and settled down to sleep, worn out from the emotional day.

*

Shelton woke with a start, confused and wondering why he was back at the brownstone. Memory flooded in, and he sat up with a glance at the bedside table. The clock assured him it was only seven in the morning. Good. He'd have time for breakfast before visiting hours started at the hospital; he was starved.

He padded naked to the kitchen and poured a bowl of cereal, sparing a scowl for the cold coffee pot. He'd forgotten to set it up the night before. Deciding caffeine was worth the wait, he added water and coffee to the machine and ate his granola while it dripped.

The rich aroma made him drool, and he quickly filled a cup. Impatient for a taste, he took a tiny sip and flinched when he burned his tongue. Damn. He carried the mug with him to cool as he dressed.

He decided on well-worn jeans and noticed how the olive flecks in the brown sweater he'd chosen brought out the green in his hazel eyes. He ran fingers through his chestnut curls, tilting his head at his reflection in the mirror. Did he need a trim?

Shelton smiled at himself and dropped his arms to his sides. He felt like a boy on his first date! Nevil wouldn't care what he wore. He gulped his coffee and then retrieved his keys from the pile of clothing on the floor along with his phone and wallet. After he packed a change of clothes for Nevil, he went to the front door, pulled on his boots, and grabbed a coat from the closet.

A chilly wind struck him as he stepped outside, and he turned up his collar on the way to the light rail train stop on the next block. Unfortunately, he had time to think about his future as the train whisked him toward the hospital. Since it was Thursday, he'd be able to contact the Human Resources department about a possible transfer back to Oregon. Pulling his phone from a pocket, he searched for the number. He'd never met the bank's District Manager, Thomas Baker, but he'd try to meet with him to salvage what he could of his career.

Distracted, he chewed his lower lip as the phone rang. Of course, he'd talk to Nevil before he made any decisions. The last choice he'd made alone had been disastrous—lesson learned. Voicemail answered, and he left his request, along with his name and number. "Please call me back. It's urgent," he asked before he ended the call.

The train came to a stop, and he followed a subdued group of people to the hospital entrance. Becoming lost in the long corridors, he chanced upon Nevil's room in time to hear his cheery laughter. He stepped through the doorway with a smile on his face and paused, for a moment thrown off balance by the handsome man that stood across the room from Nevil.

Shelton shook off his surprise and, with a quick glance at Nevil, crossed the floor to the visitor. "Hi, Percy. It's nice to see you again."

Percy gripped his hand, confusing Shelton further by placing a light kiss on his cheek. "Shelton, you're looking good. I'd think Nevil would be more careful of his neck with you in his life."

"Hey, kiss your own man," Nevil teased from the bed. Shelton looked at him, and his heart quickened with pity. Dark bruises spotted Nevil's temple and circled his beautiful eyes; his mussed black hair emphasized the white porcelain of his face. Nevil held out a hand, and Shelton went to him. Conscious of Percy at his back, he bent to kiss Nevil's cheek, but Nevil turned his head at the last second and seized Shelton's lips in a kiss he felt all the way to his toes.

Shelton eased back and willed his cock to behave as he caught sight of the loose sling around Nevil's left arm. "Good morning, honey. Doing okay?"

Nevil didn't answer. His gaze traveled from the obvious bulge in Shelton's worn jeans, up his tight sweater, to the faint flush Shelton knew colored his cheeks. The admiration in his eyes made Shelton's pulse hammer, and he gave Nevil a shy smile, glad he had dressed nice for his man.

Nevil shrugged off his question. "I'm fine. Glad you're here. Percy has an announcement for us."

"Really?" Shelton turned to Percy and tried to drum up some enthusiasm for the attractive man who'd once had Nevil's love. He watched, intrigued, as color rose in Percy's cheeks.

Percy cleared his throat. "I'm getting married," he confessed with a slightly embarrassed laugh, though his gray eyes shone with joy.

Shelton felt a grin spread on his face. Percy's happiness was contagious. "Congratulations! Who's the lucky man?"

"Do you remember Brandon Eagar?"

"What! That gorgeous young man you dated awhile back?"

"I never stopped. But it's taken me nearly two years to convince him he can't live without me."

"I'm really happy for you." Carried away by emotions he couldn't explain, Shelton left Nevil's side to embrace him. "Have you set a date?"

Percy's smile broadened. "I wanted to wait until summer when Brandon has some time off between terms, but he insists we go to New York this weekend, where his parents live, and be married immediately."

"Percy! That's great." Excited, Shelton glanced at Nevil to include him and tried to ignore the stab of disappointment on seeing Nevil's mocking smile. He knew Nevil's thoughts on marriage. Why was his heart being such a fool about it?

Nevil's eyes widened, and he gave Shelton a curious look, but his smile appeared genuine when he turned to Percy. "We'll definitely be there. I have to see this for myself."

"Oh, you'll be there, seeing as you're my best man."

Nevil blinked in surprise, unmistakably touched by the gesture. "Thank you, Percy. I'd be honored."

"Good. That's settled." Percy glanced at his watch. "Well, I'd better get to work. Shelton, please make sure Nevil doesn't fall off any roofs before my wedding?"

"I'll do my best," Shelton said dryly. They embraced again, and Percy gave Nevil a light kiss on the lips and left the room. Shelton smiled when Percy's merry whistle reached them.

"I'm happy for him," he said and met the smile in Nevil's eyes. "So, can I take you home yet?"

"The doctor's supposed to come by this morning to release me. If you lock that door, I'll dress and be ready for him."

After a glance down the near-empty hallway, Shelton closed the door and twisted the lock. Nevil had already thrown off the covers, and his feet dangled over the side of the bed. Shelton winced and hurried to him. With great care, he eased Nevil's injured arm from the sling around his neck.

"Let me help," he said unsteadily and stepped between Nevil's knees. He leaned over to untie the hospital gown at the back, and a shiver of desire raced through him as Nevil's warm breath brushed his cheek. He groaned when Nevil turned his head and nuzzled Shelton's sensitive ear and drew the lobe between his teeth.

"Oh, Lord," Shelton said, helpless. "You're not making this easy."

"I don't intend to," Nevil answered with a laugh in his voice.

He undid the last knot with shaky fingers and then drew the gown from Nevil's body. He let out a breath of dismay. Bruises covered the left side of Nevil's well-toned body, spreading in a purple and blue mass on his hip.

Nevil raised Shelton's chin with a gentle finger. "I'm fine, love. Try me and see."

Shelton's gaze dropped at once to Nevil's beautiful cock, hard and thick. Precome glistened at the tip. Drawn irresistibly to the sweet honey despite his better judgment, Shelton lowered his head to lap at it with his tongue.

"God, yes," Nevil groaned.

Nevil gripped Shelton's hair as he drew his tongue over the sensitive slit. Although aware of their limited privacy, Shelton decided to show no mercy and slid his lips and teeth over the engorged head, sucking Nevil's length into his mouth.

Nevil made no pretense of holding back and plunged into Shelton's eager lips. Encouraged, Shelton fondled his firm balls. He kneaded and squeezed them as his lips raced up and down the straining pole. At Nevil's telltale moan, Shelton relaxed his muscles and drew Nevil's cock into the back of his throat and swallowed.

Nevil's hips rose from the bed, and he moaned Shelton's name as he came, his delicious come filling Shelton's mouth and coating the back of his throat. Shelton swallowed, greedy for his lover's taste. He didn't release Nevil until he devoured every drop of the sticky nectar.

Again, Nevil raised Shelton's chin and met his lips in a kiss that made his head spin before he moved to

Shelton's ear. "I love you," he whispered. Shelton shivered as Nevil's right hand traveled down the front of his sweater and fumbled with the buttons of his jeans.

Shelton touched his wrist to stop him even though his body screamed against it. "You'd better get dressed before the doctor walks in on us."

"But I'm hungry," Nevil purred with fire in his eyes as he deftly undid the top button of Shelton's fly.

"Honey, do me later! I'd die if we got started and had to stop to let the doctor in. Please?"

Nevil studied his face, and a pleasant shudder passed through Shelton at the gleam in his beautiful eyes. He groaned when Nevil palmed his dick and stroked his aching erection through his jeans with his thumb. "Oh, I'll definitely 'do you,' love. Have no fear."

Shelton became lost in the pleasure of Nevil's skillful touch, pressing his cock into Nevil's hand. He moaned at the fire that licked his nerves when Nevil played with his balls; he forgot all about the doctor as Nevil undid another button and stroked the head of his dick.

He panicked at a soft knock on the door and jumped back from Nevil. Shit! He glared when Nevil chuckled under his breath and tossed the bag of clothing to him on his way to the door. "Put some clothes on."

Twisting the lock, he opened the door a little. "Nevil's getting dressed. Can you give us a minute?"

He felt the heat in his face when the doctor's lips twitched before he glanced at his watch. "I can come back in ten. Will that give you enough time?" he asked. His gaze flicked to the open buttons on Shelton's jeans.

"Thanks," Shelton muttered and closed the door again. He laughed at the absurdity of the moment and went to help Nevil dress.

Chapter Three

The doctor returned as promised, checked Nevil over, and discharged him.

"I left a prescription at the nurse's station for you to pick up on your way out. Pain meds for the headache I know you're hiding, and you can also take them for your arm."

"Thank you, Dr. Franklyn," Nevil said with his charming smile.

Shelton gave the love of his life a dry look. Always the flirt. He shook the doctor's hand and took the copy of the release papers from him. "Thank you for taking such good care of him. I have to tell you, it was a relief to find him here rather than in ICU."

"It was my pleasure. Take care."

Nevil collected his prescription papers at the front desk, and they made their way to the elevators. A soft rain fell as they emerged from the hospital entrance, and they dashed to the train depot. Deep in thought, Shelton chewed his lip while they waited.

He glanced at Nevil beside him and noted the white set of his lips. "I could take you home first if your head hurts. There's no reason I can't retrieve the car myself later and pick up your prescription."

Nevil gave him a smile and slipped his warm hand into Shelton's. "Let's pick it up together. I feel like I've just been released from prison. I want to be outside for a while."

"Just don't get chilled," Shelton said, and then he groaned. "I sound like a mother hen. Please ignore me. I think I left my brain back in Colorado."

Nevil chuckled. "As long as your luscious body is here," he murmured and smacked his lips together.

Shelton darted a glance around. No one paid them any attention, so he gave Nevil a light kiss and then wished he hadn't as every nerve in his body ignited. He wanted Nevil wrapped around him—now—with Nevil's gorgeous cock buried deep inside him.

He jerked his gaze down the tracks, embarrassed and aching. He hoped Nevil hadn't noticed the tremble in his hands. They would pick up the Prius, go home, and Nevil would take his meds and then go to bed. Shelton would have to content himself with a shower where he could get rid of the hard-on he'd suffered through all morning. The idea made him feel alone. Without a thought, he squeezed Nevil's hand.

Nevil leaned close to whisper in his ear, "Don't forget... You promised to let me 'do' you."

Shelton laughed, breathless. He turned back to Nevil and touched his lips with an unsteady finger. "I'm holding you to that," he said, then sucked in air when Nevil's velvet soft lips closed over his fingertip. He watched in captive fascination as his digit disappeared bit by bit between

Nevil's pale lips. He felt the roughness of Nevil's tongue in the moist, hot depths. Nevil pushed the finger to the roof of his mouth and sucked on it. God! Shelton's prick hardened more with each draw. As Nevil's tongue rolled around his finger, his balls grew tight and aching again.

"Damn, Nevil... stop! You're going to get us arrested," he panted in Nevil's ear. He was ready to drag Nevil behind the hospital and fuck him senseless.

Nevil's throaty laugh made him shiver with bliss. "The train's coming."

Shelton dropped his head on Nevil's shoulder and fought to calm his unsteady senses. Nevil didn't play fair. He could have sobbed when Nevil's body heat wrapped around him, teasing him closer when it was time to pull away.

"Come on, love. It won't take long to get the car. Then we can go home," Nevil promised as he tugged on his sleeve. Shelton boarded the sleek train car but chose to stand when Nevil patted the seat beside him. He couldn't be sure where Nevil's fingers would roam if he sat down. Nevil gave him a delighted smile in answer, reading his mind with ease. Shelton scowled and looked out the window as the train gathered speed. His wanton mind pictured Nevil's mouth on him as they swept along the tracks, and he had to stifle a moan in his throat.

They reached the downtown area in less than ten minutes and disembarked at the station closest to where Nevil had parked the Prius. The rain had stopped; Shelton took a minute to straighten Nevil's collar and zip the jacket tighter over his chest. Nevil grinned and kissed the tip of his nose. "Thanks."

"How's the elbow?" he asked. He had noticed Nevil's slight wince when he brushed the sling by accident.

"It's starting to hurt a little but nothing serious. Come on, let's get the car."

The block they walked along boasted half a dozen brick buildings that had fallen into disrepair, which Nevil's company had begun to renovate. Without warning, Nevil halted on the sidewalk in front of one of them. Shelton scowled. "Is that the one you were hurt in?"

Nevil nodded his head and studied Shelton's face. Shelton tried to smile but couldn't shake the fear he could have lost his lover and best friend yesterday if Nevil's fall had been worse. As Nevil watched him, all the mischief left his eyes to be replaced with regret.

Nevil cupped his face and sighed, and Shelton turned his head to kiss his warm palm. "I didn't mean to scare you like that," Nevil said earnestly. "It was an initial walkthrough, and I found a fabulous picture window up there. Wasn't watching my feet, obviously."

Shelton bit back the bitter words on his tongue. He wasn't about to tell Nevil how to do his job; he was a brilliant designer. If he needed to go into a dangerous building...

Shelton's anger melted away when Nevil's thumb touched his lips. Nevil teased his lips open and leaned in to brush his mouth over Shelton's. "Come here," he murmured. He pulled Shelton toward the building. Shelton didn't care where they went—anywhere, as long as he could still kiss Nevil.

Nevil pulled a ring of keys from a pocket and let them in the front entrance of the abandoned office building. He locked the door behind them, and urged Shelton through a door on the right, latching that one as well. A quick glance around the room showed Shelton a desk littered with drawings and several vacant chairs. Nevil's hand went around the back of his neck and pulled him into a kiss.

God, yes! Shelton devoured Nevil's mouth. Their tongues fenced and twined as Shelton sucked on the moist sweetness within. His senses ignited. His need for Nevil had the aspects of an animalistic lust. This was more than love. He needed to join with Nevil, tangled in a celebration of life.

His fingers dropped to Nevil's zipper, and in seconds, his hand wrapped around his sleek, hard cock. His moan echoed Nevil's. Shelton's dick thrust forward at a tug on the buttons of his jeans. He slid his free hand up Nevil's back and urged him closer as he tried to deepen their kiss.

Nevil tore his lips from Shelton's. "Goddamn, Shelton. Help me!"

Shelton blinked, dazed with want, and took in Nevil's flushed cheeks, Nevil's eyes blazing with lust and frustration.

"Sorry," he mumbled. He took tight hold of his abandoned senses. With care, he lifted the sling over Nevil's dark head and helped him out of his coat. He tossed it aside and made Nevil put the sling back on.

"You'll only try to use it otherwise," he said, distracted by the buttons on Nevil's shirt. He undid them one by one; Nevil's chest heaved as his tongue followed his fingers down his sweat-glistened muscles. He became lost in the salty taste of heated skin as he inhaled Nevil's own scent. He found a hard bud and bit it gently and then soothed it with his tongue.

His mouth traveled lower to follow the sexy line of dark hair to Nevil's open fly. Precome leaked from the delicious mushroom head of Nevil's dick. He knelt to lick at it and slipped his hands inside to cup Nevil's tight ass. Nudging the slacks down over muscular legs, he slid off Nevil's shoes.

Nevil shuddered under his touch, and Shelton grinned in triumph around Nevil's cock as he sucked on the end. Easing back, he drew his tongue along the thick vein that ran under the hard shaft and buried his nose in Nevil's tight sac. He breathed in the heated, musky scent, and his head swam. In a haze of lust, he grazed his teeth along the delicious cock that could give him so much pleasure.

Nevil's fingers threaded in his curls and urged Shelton to his feet; their lips met in a sensual kiss.

"Undress for me, baby," Nevil whispered against his mouth. The roughness of his voice sent waves of anticipation through Shelton's body. He stepped back and stripped off his sweater. Electricity shot through him when Nevil tweaked a nipple that peeked from the sparse golden curls on his chest. He kicked off his shoes, undid the buttons on his fly, and slipped off his jeans and boxer shorts. He didn't give a damn about the socks as Nevil's fingers tickled down his abdomen and gripped his aching cock.

A groan burst from his throat and rang in the room as Nevil stroked him with expertise. He wasn't going to last... Nevil dropped to his knees, swallowed Shelton's cock, and worked him with lips, tongue, and teeth.

Shelton peeked at the dark head bent over him. The sight of his cock as it pushed between Nevil's lips blew his mind. Nevil drew back, and Shelton caught a glimpse of Nevil stroking his own dick.

Fuck! Shelton's balls tightened, and he came in a burst of ecstasy, his mind lost in senseless bliss. He glanced down as his cock slipped out of Nevil's mouth. Nevil sat back on his heels. Pleasure infused his face while he stroked off. Irrational jealousy pricked Shelton, and he dropped down on all fours. He gripped Nevil's wrist to stop him and then gobbled Nevil whole, drawing the thick, hot cock to the back of his throat. He swallowed and felt the shudder that ran over Nevil's body; it burst in a tangy stream down his throat.

Shelton indulged himself a moment to suckle Nevil's dick as it softened and then sat back. Nevil met his gaze, and they grinned at each other. Shelton's heart leaped at the happiness in Nevil's lovely eyes.

Nevil picked up Shelton's hand and kissed the knuckles. "Welcome home, love."

Shelton felt the blush of pleasure in his cheeks. He liked the soft, sated look on Nevil's face. For a second he pretended they were married and that Nevil wanted only him for the rest of his life.

He laughed a little at his fancy and tugged on Nevil's hand. "Come on, hon; let's go home."

Shelton took delight in dressing Nevil despite his darling's grumbles and then threw on his own clothes while Nevil unlocked the door. They walked with clasped hands from the building, oblivious to the stares from the few pedestrians they passed on the sidewalk. Shelton started in surprise when his phone buzzed in his pocket.

He pulled Nevil to a stop when he saw who had called. "Just a second. I need to hear this." A frown grew between his brows as he listened to the voice message. Glancing at his watch, he turned in a panic to Nevil when the recording ended. "I have to get you home! I have an appointment with the bank's district manager in less than an hour."

Nevil glowered. "An interview?"

Shelton winced, though he deserved the suspicion. He picked up Nevil's hand again and played with his fingers. "I was going to discuss it with you this time. I don't want to be apart from you any longer. Enough is enough. I'm seeing what the bank can do for me out here. I'm not going back to Colorado, even if it means finding a job with someone else. If you'd like that," he amended.

He kept his gaze on Nevil's face, and his heart tripped with uncertainty when Nevil chewed on his kiss-swollen bottom lip. Nevil leaned close and put his mouth against Shelton's ear. "Good. I fucking hate sleeping without you."

Shelton let out his held breath in a relieved sigh. "I was hoping you'd say that. Let's go. I need to change out of these jeans."

"The car's this way," Nevil said and led him to the nearby parking garage. They made a quick drive home, beating the afternoon traffic. Shelton settled Nevil in bed for a nap and then dressed and returned to the Prius. He preferred to take the light rail into town, but time was pressing. He maneuvered the car onto the street, trying to ignore the knot of worry in his stomach as he crossed the city to learn his future.

Chapter Four

A gust of wind and rain struck Shelton the instant he stepped outside the glass doors of the office building. He made a conscious effort not to worry his already abused bottom lip with his teeth, setting his briefcase down to pull a cap out of his coat pocket. That's that.

"Damn," he muttered, irritated when the breeze lifted his curls and sent raindrops down the back of his neck. He wished he'd been more prepared for the meeting with Mark Baker. As it was, he hadn't stayed professionally aloof. He'd fallen into the quicksand and made a personal plea, doomed to fail.

He crammed the hat on his head and trotted across the plaza to the coffee shop on the corner. Cold and wet, he needed a hot drink to brace against the discouragement that weighed on his shoulders. The shop was comfortable, warm, and smelled of fresh coffee and cinnamon. He ordered an espresso and took a small table at the window.

Chin on his hand, Shelton watched the rain slide down the glass. *I should have expected it.* Baker had gone over some paperwork with him when he'd first entered the district manager's office and had thrown him for a loop when he asked Shelton if he was single or married.

"Just filling in the blanks." Baker showed him the section he'd overlooked. Shelton had blinked at him. Boyfriend... partner... what the hell was Nevil? At last he mumbled that he was single and felt miserable about it afterwards.

The interview had gone downhill from there. Mark had been polite and sympathetic, but in the end had to disappoint Shelton.

"The only opening we have in the area is in Gresham in the Loan Department. I realize that's going backwards for you but..."

Of course Shelton had taken the position. Damn it. Back to square one with no prospects for the future. He smiled when the barista set the espresso at his elbow, though his thoughts ran in circles. Wistful, he stared into the black liquid in the small cup as he thought of Nevil and the question on the application. Another dream out of reach.

This one hurt though. Sure, he was Nevil's boyfriend, but Nevil had dated lots of men. He'd even lived with a few of them once upon a time. But none of them had ever had the right to call him husband. Hot blood flooded his face. God, he wanted that. He wanted the privilege to call Nevil his husband.

His hand shook when he drank the double shot he'd ordered. With care, he set the cup down, opened his briefcase, and took out his laptop. Speaking of weddings, he'd better book their flight and hotel for Albany, New York, if they were to leave at a decent hour tomorrow.

The irony wasn't lost on him. "I'll probably feel better when this weekend is over," he muttered as the computer booted up. His phone buzzed, and he glanced at the text message, a grin tugging his lips. A note from Paul Benson lit the screen, a friend from the bank in Colorado, asking how the interview went. Having his own challenges with his youthful boyfriend, Paul and he had spent many an evening commiserating over their complicated relationships. It seemed things were working out for Paul and Eran now. He smiled, happy for them, and Eran even did some modeling for Tera. He wondered if he and Nevil would have such a happy ending.

Shelton sighed and put the phone back in his pocket. He'd send a message when his mood improved. It didn't take long to make the reservations he needed and then log off. Gathering his things, he turned up the collar of his coat against the rain and made his way to the parking garage to retrieve the Prius. He'd grown anxious to get home and see how Nevil fared.

*

Shelton's spirits rose on the short ride home. He had good news for Nevil. Even if the job at the bank wasn't what he'd hoped for, at least he wouldn't have to return to Denver except to pack. As he turned the Prius into the driveway and shut off the engine, he wondered if Nevil would feel up to a celebration.

Shelton tried to be quiet as he entered the brownstone and then smiled and tossed his coat and keys on the side table by the door when he spotted Nevil on the living room couch. He didn't wear the sling for his arm; it must feel better. Shelton walked across the room and looked down at him. "Hey, baby."

"Hi." Nevil glanced at the wall clock. "That didn't take long."

"No, but I have good news." Shelton sat close to him, making sure his thigh brushed against Nevil's. "Looks like you're going to have a roommate again."

All of Shelton's doubts dissolved at the delighted smile that covered Nevil's face. "They're transferring you?"

"Not exactly... I get my old position back at a different branch of the bank. But it's better than being out of a job."

Shelton made sure to smile when Nevil studied his face. Nevil cupped his cheek with a warm palm and kissed him. "I'm sorry. I know you wanted that promotion."

Shelton shrugged. "I did want it, but the price is too high. These last seven months have been hell, and now that you're no longer doing any consulting work in Colorado, it's been even worse. I want to come home."

"Thank God," Nevil said fervently. He kissed him, a gentle caress that lingered and expressed his love and joy more than words. He shifted on the couch and deepened the kiss. Shelton pulled him gently into his arms.

They both swore when the doorbell rang, shattering the moment.

"Tell whoever it is to go the fuck away," Nevil called after him when Shelton crossed the room to answer it. Shelton was still laughing when he opened the door and saw Tera's smile. She held two zippered cases in her arms, which he took as she stepped into the foyer out of the rain.

"Hi again," she said cheerfully and kissed his cheek.

"Hi, yourself. What's all this?"

"Percy stopped by the shop and picked out Nevil's tuxedo for the wedding," she explained as she removed her coat and joined her brother in the living room. She returned her twin's scowl with a syrupy smile as she sat beside him. "I thought he should try it on in case I need to alter the length or make another adjustment."

Nevil eyed the bags in Shelton's arms with interest. "Which one did he choose?"

"He and Brandon are wearing white and picked out the pearl gray for you."

"Oh, I love that one." Nevil stood and took the bag with his name on it from Shelton.

Shelton held up the other one with curiosity. "And this?"

Tera smiled. "I chose a suit for you, if you don't mind. The charcoal gray one we shot pictures of last month."

Nevil looked outraged. "You mean the one that brings out the green in his eyes and makes them seem enormous? It's way too sexy for that crowd. No way am I letting him loose in a room full of hot young blades while I'm stuck at Percy's side."

Shelton laughed, though he tingled with pleasure at the compliment. "I promise I won't flirt with anyone at the wedding but you."

Nevil looked ready to argue and then shrugged. "Give me a minute to try this on," he muttered and left the room with a sniff.

Shelton smiled after him and then laid his own suit over the arm of a chair and sat beside Tera on the couch. "Were you able to get tickets for the same flight as ours?"

"Yes, but not in first class. We're somewhere back by the bathrooms."

"Oh, that's tough. Maybe we can switch off with you and Robert for part of the flight."

"Deal."

They both looked up when Nevil walked into the room, and Shelton hoped Tera hadn't heard his sharp inhalation. Nevil always looked good in a suit. The soft material of the gray slacks caressed his muscular thighs as he approached them and drew Shelton's eyes upwards to the deliciously full groin area.

Nevil had left the pristine white dress shirt unbuttoned, and Shelton's gaze continued its journey. He adored the sparse curls on Nevil's sculpted stomach and chest. Nevil's honey-colored tan looked incredible against the light material. Shelton ached to lick his way from Nevil's navel to his chin, to linger on the dark buds that peeked on the edges of the dress shirt.

Nevil winked at him, and Shelton felt the heat of a blush in his face and furtively rearranged his cock when Tera rose to her feet.

She ran a critical gaze over Nevil. "The pants seem long. Shelton, would you mind folding the cuffs under for me?" Shelton knelt at Nevil's feet and rolled a cuff higher. Tera chewed her lips. "No, I think they're good the way they are. Thank you, Shelton."

"Anytime." Shelton sat back on his heels. His heated gaze traveled up Nevil's leg and lingered on the bulge at the zipper. Nevil coughed, and Shelton raised his eyes. His lips parted at the desire in the blue-green depths that looked down at him.

Tera's indulgent laugh recalled him, and Shelton scrambled to his feet as she crossed the room and picked up her purse from the side table. She grinned at him over her shoulder. "I can see I'm no longer needed here. Goodnight, darlings. I'll see you at the airport—nine sharp."

"Goodnight, dear." Shelton followed her to the door and kissed her cheek, making sure she got in her car safely and drove away before he locked the door behind her. He grunted in surprise when Nevil shoved him from behind and pinned him against the door with his body. He nuzzled Shelton's neck and moved his head to nibble at an earlobe.

Shelton lifted his shoulder. "That tickles! How are you feeling?" Stupid question with Nevil's thick length pushing against his ass. Nevil's chuckle vibrated along his nerves, and Shelton's semi-erect dick twitched in response, eager to swell.

"What do you think?" Nevil murmured and guided Shelton's hand between them. His fingers brushed against Nevil's cock, and he squeezed the exciting thickness. He stroked the warm shaft and enjoyed the silky glide of fabric over its hardness. Nevil's sharp breath and moan in his ear sent Shelton's pulse racing.

Nevil's skillful fingers loosened Shelton's tie and undid buttons in a flash to bare his chest. Shelton jumped when Nevil tweaked his nipples on their way lower, loving the sting that zipped straight to his dick. He leaned back in Nevil's arms and cupped Nevil's heavy balls, distracted as his own belt and zipper were undone. Nevil dipped a hand into Shelton's boxers, and he groaned when Nevil fished out his erect cock.

He leaned his head back and twisted to meet Nevil's greedy kiss. Nevil stroked and squeezed Shelton's cock and pleasure burst through him, Nevil thumbing the head of his dick on each pass. Nevil murmured a few words he didn't catch, and Shelton staggered when Nevil stepped back from him.

"Sorry, love," Nevil apologized with a laugh in his voice. "I need the room."

Shelton thrilled at the joy in Nevil's voice. God, they were good together! With a quick tug, Nevil whisked off Shelton's pants and boxers and slipped off his shirt.

"Leave the tie," he said as he batted Shelton's hands away. In a playful gesture, he slapped his ass. "Spread 'em, hon."

Shelton swallowed as a jolt of lust left his mouth dry. He loved it when Nevil took control. It left him free to enjoy whatever pleasures Nevil's nimble mind came up with. He turned and placed his hands over his head against the door, feet apart.

Nevil's hands rested lightly on Shelton's hips, and he felt a warm breath and a soft caress on his neck. He shivered, goose bumps breaking out over his flesh as Nevil gave a long, slow lick down his spine. His lips lingered at the small of Shelton's back, little kisses sending sparks of flame over his nerves. Nevil's tongue darted in and out of the start of his crack and drove him crazy with anticipation.

Shelton bit his lip in frustration when Nevil raised his head and moved back from him again. Missing the warmth of Nevil's body, he glanced over his shoulder. Nevil had removed his dress shirt, and Shelton saw him wince and rub his left elbow before hanging it over the back of the chair at the side table.

Shelton left his position when Nevil fumbled one-handed with his belt. "Let me help you," he said. He ignored Nevil's protest and slipped his arms around Nevil's waist, cupping his muscular ass.

"You were supposed to stay at the door," Nevil chided, and then he groaned when Shelton nipped a dark bud on his chest. Shelton soothed it with his tongue and drew another moan from his darling when he rubbed it between his lips.

"I got lonely," he said and kissed his way up Nevil's delicious skin to the warm soft spot under his jaw. His dick throbbed, and with a sudden worry he might stain the light material he rubbed against, he undid Nevil's belt and lowered his slacks.

"Good idea. At least one of us is thinking," Nevil said and held onto Shelton's shoulder as he knelt and helped him out of his pants and the dark briefs he favored. Shelton thrust the pants into Nevil's hands, distracted by the freed cock at his eye level. Nevil's dick curved upwards toward his stomach; his balls were heavy and tight beneath. Shelton pushed his nose against Nevil's sac and breathed deeply of the musky skin.

He licked the seam between Nevil's balls and nearly bit Nevil's finger when he slipped it under his chin and forced him to look up. Nevil's turquoise eyes gleamed with passion and laughter, and he raked his fingers through Shelton's curls.

"Can I fuck you now?" he asked and lifted a dark brow.

"Just getting you ready, dear." Shelton dropped his gaze back to Nevil's gorgeous dick. He smiled at the soft chuckle he heard.

Shelton licked the glistening head of Nevil's cock, loving how it jumped. He captured it with his lips and groaned along with Nevil as he sucked it in and the head slid along the roof of his mouth to fill him. Nevil tried to draw back, but Shelton grabbed his ass. He relaxed his throat and nudged Nevil in further and swallowed around the head. He swallowed again; he wanted to swallow Nevil whole, but he needed to breathe.

Irritation flashed through him when Nevil took advantage of his loosened hold and pulled out, then tugged on Shelton's hair to get him to stand. Nevil rested his forehead against Shelton's and breathed just as hard, his face flushed and eyes wild with desire. He nipped Shelton's lower lip. "I want to come in your ass, not down your throat," he pleaded.

A thrill of power shivered along Shelton's spine at the insistent note in Nevil's voice. Nevil seldom begged. A sure sign he hovered on the edge of control.

"Whatever you say," Shelton teased. He reached around Nevil for the drawer in the side table by the front door. Where was... He frowned at the nearly empty tube he found under a stack of papers and then shrugged, squeezing what remained of the lubricant into his hand. It seemed enough for what he had in mind. He grinned at Nevil's impatient hiss.

"Ready?" he mocked and smoothed the gel over Nevil's rigid cock, enjoying the glide of the thick shaft in his slick palm. He glanced up through his lashes at Nevil's murmurs of pleasure. Nevil's intent gaze followed his hand, and Shelton moved closer and rubbed their cocks together. He slid his hand over his own dick and thrilled at Nevil's quickly drawn breath. When he met Nevil's heated glance, he enjoyed a few more strokes and then reached around and slid his fingers down the crack of his own ass.

He dipped a slippery finger into his hole. *Damn, that feels good.* Shelton closed his eyes and wondered if Nevil knew how ready and willing he wanted to be fucked. He shoved a second finger in, impatient as he reached for that one spot...

He moaned aloud as lips closed around the head of his dick and sucked him into the liquid fire of Nevil's mouth.

Fuck! Too good. Pleasure radiated from his expertly played cock as Nevil sucked and licked and swallowed him down. Frantic, Shelton shoved his fingers in and out of his hole as pressure built in his balls. Then Nevil slid an unexpected finger inside him as well, pushing him to the edge as he massaged the tight ring of muscles that guarded Shelton's passage.

Nevil's throat constricted around the head of his cock, and Shelton whimpered at the bliss that spiraled down his nerves. Nevil's free hand fondled his swollen balls, and Shelton lost control and cried out as pleasure surged from his dick down Nevil's throat.

"Stop," he begged as Nevil continued to suckle him. Every nerve twitched at the pull on his sensitive cock. At last, Nevil released him and withdrew his finger from Shelton's ass. He stood and pushed Shelton back toward the front door.

Shelton was lightheaded, and his nerves tingled when he turned and braced his arms against the solid wood. Nevil lined up and shoved into him with little resistance. This was what he lived for! His moans echoed Nevil's, and he gasped for air as he drowned in the incredible sensation of Nevil's cock thrusting deep inside him. Tears stung his eyes, and love swelled in his chest to tangle with his lust.

He shouted in surprised ecstasy when Nevil shifted position and hit his prostate.

"There we are," Nevil murmured, voice thick, and leaned over him. He braced an arm on the wall next to Shelton's head and proceeded to drive him crazy with each slide of his dick over his sensitive spot.

Shelton hardened again, and he groped blindly between his legs. His fingers brushed his cock and balls to close around Nevil's sac. Nevil's balls tightened in his hand, and his cry rang in Shelton's ear as he came in quick jerks.

Shelton grabbed his own dick and, in a few hard pulls, joined Nevil, eyes shut as he rode out the intense orgasm.

He heard Nevil chuckle when he could think again, and he straightened and turned into Nevil's warm embrace. Nevil's grin covered his face, and he touched Shelton's cheek, his eyes bright. "You're amazing. Small wonder I love you so much."

Shelton's heart stuck in his throat. Unable to speak, he twined his fingers around Nevil's neck and kissed him instead. He basked in Nevil's murmurs of approval. Nevil kept his arm around Shelton's waist when their lips parted. With a glance over Shelton's shoulder, he tugged on his hand.

"Come on, love. Let's shower. We'll clean up later."

"Sound good to me," Shelton sighed, content to let Nevil lead him to the bedroom. They showered and afterwards, deciding a nap took precedence, snuggled together on their bed. Shelton gave a contented sigh. This was where he wanted to be, held tight in Nevil's arms. It didn't take long for Nevil's soft snores to fill the silence in the room and Shelton rose up on an elbow to look at him in the faint light filtering through the curtains. A smile curled Nevil's full lips.

"What are you thinking?" Shelton whispered, gently brushing Nevil's bangs off his face. He knew Nevil loved him, but he often wondered what went on in that clever mind of his.

"Would be fascinating to know," he murmured and nestled against Nevil's side, his heavy lids fluttering closed as he drifted off into sleep.

Chapter Five

Nevil woke from a wonderful dream that involved Shelton, and he smiled at the warmth of the body pressed against his back. After their nap yesterday, they'd spent a quiet evening watching TV and had an early night. Shelton shifted against him, and Nevil grinned. Damn, he'd missed this! He'd woken up alone far too many mornings. He'd been furious with Shelton when he took that position in Colorado for the simple, selfish reason that he hated to sleep in an empty bed. Thank God that was over.

He rolled onto his back and winced at the stab of pain in his left elbow. How long did bruises take to heal, anyway? Altogether tired of hurting.

Shelton sighed in his sleep, and Nevil turned to him. Love flooded his heart. *He's so damned sexy!* Shelton's full lips parted a little, with a hint of moisture in the corner that Nevil had the sudden urge to lick away. Dark lashes and a few stray curls hid his eyes. Nevil counted the smatter of freckles on his cheeks–still eight.

The clock pinged on the bedside table, and Shelton stirred and murmured a few incoherent words. Nevil reached across him to turn off the alarm and then leaned on his elbow to watch his eyelashes flicker. This was his favorite moment. Shelton's lids opened, and hazel eyes gave him a sleepy stare. He blinked. Affection and awareness entered Shelton's gaze. A smile spread on his face, though he reddened under Nevil's scrutiny. "Hi."

"Hey, baby." Nevil lowered his head, unable to resist the temptation of Shelton's mouth. First, the slight bitterness of a morning kiss, but then Shelton's own sweet taste drowned it out. Nevil lingered over the intimacy, their tongues sliding together. He drew back to tease Shelton's sleep-softened lips, and Shelton groaned and plunged his tongue deep into Nevil's mouth. He sucked Nevil's tongue. Nevil's dick responded, hardening in an instant.

Yes! Fire swept through him and he nipped Shelton's lower lip and then sat up and threw the blankets off. He nodded in approval at Shelton's thick cock, aroused and arching toward his stomach, ready for Nevil's touch. Nevil licked his dry lips as he stroked a thumb over the glistening tip and then down the engorged shaft. He shuddered with a burst of lust and recalled the unparalleled pleasure of the scar tissue as it slid up his ass and over his prostate. Shelton's dick had a remarkable roughness that none of his previous lovers had matched, no matter how fancy the condom.

He glanced up to share his delight, but Shelton wouldn't meet his gaze. His eyes focused on Nevil's hand on his cock. "Shelton?"

Shelton looked at him, his smile strained. "I wish I was beautiful for you," he confessed on a sigh.

Nevil snorted. "Fuck beauty. You're fucking hot," he exclaimed and bent to nibble the wet head.

Shelton pushed urgently on his shoulder. "We don't have time—Nevil! The plane…"

Nevil growled in his throat and climbed Shelton's body, capturing his gaze as he gripped their dicks together in his hand. Shelton widened his eyes, and then his lashes fluttered, pretty color flooding his face from unmistakable pleasure. Triumph flashed over Nevil. Shelton was the sweetest lover he'd ever had, his best friend, capturing Nevil's elusive heart years ago.

It thrilled him no end to be the one Shelton chose to have in his bed. He'd seen the way men looked at him, his unruly curls, big hazel eyes, and shy smile a devastating combination made all the better since Shelton seemed unaware of his allure.

Nevil gripped their cocks tighter, the roughness of Shelton's dick against his own as they thrust together into his hand ramping up his pleasure. Shelton's lips parted on a groan, and Nevil seized them in a kiss, sliding his tongue into the sweet warmth of his mouth.

Shelton enveloped their cocks with his own hand, adding pressure, and Nevil came without warning, the orgasm exploding from him in hot waves of pleasure. Shelton jerked beneath him, and the warmth of his semen joined Nevil's between them. Nevil collapsed into Shelton's arms and buried his face against his neck, fighting to catch his breath. All too soon, Shelton nudged his shoulder.

"We'd better get going if we don't want to miss our flight."

"If you say so." Nevil sat up, resentful of anything that made him leave Shelton's embrace. Shelton smiled at his obvious reluctance and licked Nevil's come from his fingers. Fire scorched Nevil's veins. Hell! No way would he sleep that night until he first tasted Shelton's delicious orgasm in his mouth. A promise he intended to keep.

Shelton caught his glance, and a blush stained his face. "Um... the time?" he said, breathless.

Mischief sprang into Nevil's heart; he couldn't help it. "We could always cancel our flight," he said and trailed his fingers over Shelton's chest. He tweaked a hard nipple and grinned at Shelton's gasp, then teased at Shelton's lips with his own. "Come on, love. Percy and Brandon don't need us at their ridiculous ceremony."

Shelton stiffened, and Nevil drew back to see his face, surprised by the anger in his eyes. "What?"

He moved when Shelton pushed him off and climbed to his feet. "It means something to them," he mumbled and stalked across the room to the closet.

"Sure. I just don't see the point. They've already been living together for years."

Shelton shrugged and disappeared into the bathroom. Nevil heard the water start for the shower and followed him, not sure what he'd said to set Shelton off.

Shelton's mood seemed to lift as they showered, and he teased Nevil with little kisses on his neck while they dressed. He chatted about work and what he expected at the bank Monday while they packed, then held Nevil's hand on the light rail train to the airport. Nevil watched him closely. Something seemed to be bothering his boyfriend. Shelton's voice held a desperate note of cheeriness. Nevil frowned, afraid to speculate what it meant.

They had a cup of coffee at the airport, and Nevil let out a relieved breath when he spotted Tera and Robert across the terminal.

"Hello, darling," he said, half-rising from his chair to kiss his sister as she bent to him. "Robert." He shook his brother-in-law's hand.

"Are we ready for this?" Robert asked him as they pulled up chairs to the table.

"I can't believe Percy will settle down to one man."

"You did," Tera pointed out.

Nevil glanced at Shelton and couldn't help the slow grin that spread on his face. "I had the best of reasons," he murmured and enjoyed the flush that stained Shelton's perfect complexion. Adorable! His prick perked up. In silence, he counted the hours before he'd have Shelton alone in their hotel room.

Shelton cleared his throat and tuned to Robert. "How's business?"

"A little slow."

Robert worked as an investment broker for one of the larger shoe companies. Nevil quirked a brow at Tera as he and Shelton fell into an ongoing discussion on capital gains. Tera returned his amused smile and leaned toward him. "Over my head."

Nevil nodded in agreement, but he listened with pride as Shelton spoke knowledgeably and with confidence to the other man. Brains and beauty, what more could a man want in a... husband? Nevil frowned into his coffee cup. Is that what's wrong? Did Shelton want to get married? Shit.

He rose to his feet with the others when their flight was called and filed onto the plane deep in thought. He sighed as he settled into the first-class seat. Shelton followed Robert further down the aisle, and Tera laughed as she slipped into the seat beside him. "Guess I'm with you until they solve the world's financial crisis."

Nevil gave her an absent smile and ordered a glass of wine from the stewardess as she passed by. Tera touched his arm. "What is it?"

How much to say? "I think Shelton wants to get married," he blurted out, appalled all over again with the idea.

"Is that all?" Tera leaned her head back on the high cushion of her seat. "We've known that for ages."

"Seriously? I had no idea..." Nevil ran a hand over his hair. "This weekend is a nightmare. I have no desire to marry anyone."

"Shelton knows that. Really Nevil, what's bugging you? Anyone with half a brain can see that he's nuts about you, but he also respects your opinion in the matter too much to ever bring it up."

"But this whole marriage thing with Percy... I'm afraid he *will* mention it. Then what do I do? I wouldn't hurt him for the world."

"You might say yes and count yourself lucky."

"Lucky. Yeah. Some meaningless slip of paper will make me lucky."

"It's not meaningless to Shelton."

Nevil let out a frustrated breath. "I don't get it."

Tera shifted in her seat and gave him a hard look. "How many men did you date before Shelton? Twenty?

Fifty? A hundred? I bet you can't name them all. And a few of them were boyfriends. I think Shelton wants the right to call you husband. Something none of them could do. Something of his own. But don't worry! He knows how you feel and won't say anything. I find that very sad."

"Whatever," Nevil grumbled and slid lower in his seat, closing his eyes to shut her out. Hell. The engines rumbled; Nevil gripped his armrests as the plane taxied, gained speed, and soared into the sky. He hoped he could sleep for at least part of the long flight. Anything to avoid his twin's barbed remarks.

Chapter Six

Nevil sat up when he heard Shelton's familiar tread by his chair and returned his smile as he exchanged places with Tera. Shelton kissed his cheek. "Sorry, I lost track of time."

"No worries." Nevil signaled to the stewardess. "Will you have a drink?"

"A beer sounds good." Shelton ordered when the attendant came over.

Nevil played with the chestnut curls around Shelton's ear. Shelton lifted a shoulder and chuckled. "That tickles."

They both looked up at a soft hello. Two young men leaned toward them from their seats across the aisle. The pretty blond pointed to the magazine in his hand; Nevil didn't like the excitement in his eyes as they raked over Shelton. "Is this you?"

"Um... sure," Shelton said. "Where'd you get that?"

"It's in the seat." The blond's dark-haired friend showed them the cover to the flight magazine. Nevil snatched a copy from the pocket in front of him and flipped to the picture of Shelton.

Shelton leaned on his shoulder to look at it. "I like Tera's brown suit better," he observed and sat back. Nevil scrutinized the picture that advertised his sister's clothing line. The gray tweed set off Shelton's broad shoulders, but the sexy smirk added a touch of decadence to the otherwise sedate business suit.

"What are you smiling at?" he asked, frowning.

Shelton looked at the glossy picture again. "Oh, Jacob was making faces at me behind the camera."

"Who?"

Shelton pointed to a name below his, and Nevil turned to the mentioned article. A green-eyed beauty flirted with him from the page. The black blazer he wore was a new design, but Nevil couldn't get past the handsome face that could fuel many a fantasy.

He coughed to clear his throat. "You know him?"

"Sure. Tera uses him when I'm too busy or if she has a special look just for him."

"I could use him," Nevil muttered and then bit his tongue. He'd gotten into bad habits while Shelton had been away. He shot Shelton a look from under his lashes to encounter a laugh in Shelton's eyes.

"Sorry, darling. He only likes girls." Shelton took the magazine from him and put it away. Nevil felt the heat in his face and glared at the young men when they giggled and whispered together. They turned abruptly back to the magazine. Out of sorts and embarrassed, Nevil folded his arms on his chest, leaned his head back on the seat, and closed his eyes. Maybe he could sleep…

He had just dozed off when soft lips nibbled at his, and he relaxed and opened his mouth to Shelton's gentle assault. The kiss ended all too soon, and Nevil had the need to adjust his dick. He smiled. That would give the boys across the way something to ogle! He sighed and found Shelton's hand. As he settled deeper into the cushions, he let the noise from the engines lull him to sleep.

Nevil woke up with a crick in his neck and rubbed the ache as he sat up in his seat. Where was Shelton? He glanced around the first-class section and spotted him leaning against the wall near the bathrooms. Nevil's eyes narrowed. Shelton chatted with the two young men from across the aisle, and Nevil didn't like the way the pretty blond stood too close to him while they talked. If they sought to initiate Shelton into the Mile High Club...

He settled back in his seat and laughed at his twinge of jealousy. That's what comes from being separated for long periods of time. Maybe he should just marry him... No, either you were committed to someone, or you weren't. A slip of paper wouldn't change that.

At that moment, the seat belt sign chimed overhead. Nevil glanced at his watch. Good, they should land in less than twenty minutes. He scrutinized Shelton's face when he sat down but didn't spot any sign he'd kissed anyone he shouldn't have.

"It's been a long flight," he answered Shelton's puzzled gaze as he leaned over to kiss him. "Buckle in."

The plane landed without incident, and they shared a taxi ride to the hotel with Tera and Robert. Tera stopped him as Nevil used the key card to unlock their door.

"Do you want to meet downstairs for a snack before the rehearsal?"

Nevil looked at his watch. "You go ahead. We'll catch up with you at the church," he told them before Shelton could say anything.

Shelton lifted a brow but followed him through the doorway without comment. Nevil leaned back against the door after it closed. He'd indulged in a fantasy on the taxi ride from the airport; he and Shelton having sex while the two young men from the plane had to watch. A shiver traveled his spine, excited and aroused and not about to waste it.

Shelton reddened under his stare and glanced at his watch. "Two hours," he warned, and then he pulled his shirt over his head. Nevil's heart thumped and raced as Shelton kicked off his shoes, undid his belt and zipper, and stepped out of his slacks with obvious intent. His briefs went next. Nevil licked his lips at the blatant erection that curved toward his flat stomach.

"On the bed. All fours," he commanded.

Light flared in Shelton's eyes, and Nevil thrilled at the provocative smile that touched his full lips. "Whatever you say." Shelton inclined his head. Grabbing up his pack from the luggage, he crossed the room, bypassing the bed to reach the bathroom. Nevil snatched the lube from his overnight kit and hurried to the bed.

He fumbled with buttons as he stripped out of his clothes and then sat cross-legged at the foot of the bed to wait for Shelton. He licked his dry lips. Shelton had the most gorgeous ass... Heat swept through him when the water turned on in the bathroom, and he had trouble not touching himself, knowing Shelton was getting ready for him.

Shelton returned in short order, flicking Nevil a glance before climbing up on the bed and facing away from him, presenting his ass. Nevil thrilled at the smirk on Shelton's face. He sat up on his heels and slid both hands down Shelton's back, pausing a moment to squeeze the firm, mounded globes of his ass. Catching his breath in anticipation, he lifted and separated them to expose the puckered opening of Shelton's glorious hole. Lust shot through him and boiled his blood. He licked down the deep cleft and swirled his tongue over the tight barrier. *Oh my.* Shelton smelled of mild soap and tasted like peaches.

Nevil worked his tongue inside him, and Shelton shuddered and collapsed onto his elbows, stifling his groans in the pillows. Nevil pushed in deeper, Shelton so warm, and tight, and delicious. Shelton moaned again, and Nevil reached a hand to cup his heavy balls, kneading them gently as his tongue continued its assault. Shelton whimpered with pleasure. And then it became not enough for Nevil. He needed to be inside Shelton—now.

He groped for the lube and squeezed it onto his fingers with a shaky hand. He circled the puckered hole with the tip of a lubed finger and then nudged it inside. Instantly, a muscle clamped around it, and Nevil moaned with Shelton as he imagined that heat around his dick. He pushed a second finger in and massaged his opening, frantic to loosen the ring of muscles.

"Please..."

Shelton's strained plea undid him. He withdrew his fingers and hurried to smear his sensitive cock with the lubricant. He rose to his knees and lined up and then sank into Shelton's hot passage. He groaned as the tightness folded around him. *God damn, I love this man!*

Shelton moved restlessly, and Nevil pushed into him. He tried different angles until Shelton's sharp gasp told him he'd found the spot. He pumped with abandon, needing more. Nevil wanted all of him. He reached around for Shelton's cock and batted at the hand already there.

"Mine," he growled and took over to stroke the thick member in time with his thrusts. Shelton's quick laugh and gasp of bliss undid him. Nevil bucked as his orgasm emptied into Shelton's ass in a few hot bursts while his mind whirled into ecstasy.

Shelton shuddered under him while hot semen spilled through Nevil's fingers, and Nevil bit his shoulder when Shelton's muscles convulsed around his sensitive prick. Shelton sank onto the mattress, and Nevil went with him, spooning as they caught their breath.

Nevil brushed Shelton's damp curls aside to kiss his neck. Shelton turned in his arms, and Nevil's heart swelled at the expression in the wide, vulnerable eyes that showed a depth of love that shook him.

"Darling," he murmured in a broken breath and gave Shelton long, languid kisses straight from his full heart. Shelton stirred first, but Nevil knew their time was up and reluctantly released him.

They showered and dressed for the evening. Shelton leaned over Nevil's shoulder as he fixed his red tie in the mirror and loosened it, then undid the top two buttons of his white dress shirt. He met Nevil's eyes in the mirror. "Definitely sexy," he explained.

Nevil smiled when Shelton stepped back from him and tried to flatten his curls with his hands but gave up with a sigh. "I should have had the barber cut them off last time."

"If you do, I'll never have sex with you again," Nevil told him as he stood. He looked at Shelton's reflection; he was dressed casual, in jeans and a beige polo shirt. The chestnut curls fell in soft tendrils around his pretty face and lovely hazel eyes. Delicious.

"I could eat you alive," he said. He smacked Shelton's ass as he passed him on the way to the door and laughed under his breath at Shelton's sputtered indignation. They held hands in the elevator, and Nevil grinned when Shelton gave his fingers a squeeze. His heart expanded. *He* put that contented, happy expression on Shelton's face.

They shared a few discreet kisses in the backseat of the taxi, but Nevil sobered when they arrived and stepped onto the sidewalk in front of the renovated gothic church where the ceremony would take place. He shot a glance at Shelton, who looked just as serious. Shit. He hoped the rehearsal would go smoothly so they could get past it and on to the dinner.

Tera met them inside the door. "They're ready for you," she told Nevil. She took Shelton's hand. Nevil snorted. As if Shelton might run away. They passed up the center aisle between the ornate, carved pews. Tera's heels clicked on the tiled floor. Percy and Brandon stood at the altar railing with another man. Nevil walked straight up to his old friend and pulled him into a tight hug.

"So, you're really going through with it," he teased and thrust out his hand to Brandon when Percy grinned. He admired the young man's slight build and the serious expression on his attractive face. Percy had done well. "I don't know if you remember me."

"Of course, thank you for coming. These are my friends, Beth and George." Brandon introduced the couple who came over from admiring the stained-glass windows. "Oh, and Reverend Louis is kind enough to officiate for us," he continued as he indicated the casually dressed man with them. "My parents will meet us at the restaurant."

Nevil shook the man's hand, but his gaze slid to Shelton standing behind them with Tera. Brandon's face brightened when he saw him, and after exchanging greetings, he drew Shelton aside for a whispered conversation. What was that about?

"Shall we take our places?" the reverend invited in a pleasant tone. Nevil stood beside Percy, but stopped Shelton when he and Brandon returned and Shelton made to join the others.

"Girl talk," Shelton said at his curious look. He laughed when Nevil frowned and leaned to whisper in his ear. "He wanted advice on how to deal with such a distinctly dominant male."

Delight flared through Nevil. "Do I dominate you, love?" he asked in his most seductive voice.

Shelton's grin widened. "When I let you, dear," he quipped and bit Nevil's lower lip before he dodged out of reach. His laughter floated back to Nevil as he took a seat beside Tera and Robert in the front pew.

The simple ceremony spoke of love and commitment. Nevil didn't quite listen to the words, more interested in the expressions that crossed Brandon's face. The young man's entire focus seemed to be on Percy. He spoke when he needed to but never took his eyes off the other man. When they reached the exchange of vows, Nevil unconsciously tongued the swollen part of his lip where Shelton had bitten him. He didn't see anything magical...

Then he did see it. His heart lurched at the love and joy that animated Brandon's face as he pretended to slip a gold band on Percy's finger. Even though the official ceremony didn't take place until tomorrow, Nevil knew Brandon had just given himself—heart and soul—to his lover.

The same intense happiness suffused Percy's face as he turned to Nevil to imitate the retrieval of his ring for Brandon. Dear Lord. This was what he denied Shelton. In that instant, Nevil wanted with all his heart to bring that look of elation to Shelton's eyes.

He glanced at the pews to share his discovery with Shelton and found the spot next to Tera empty. Tera's eyes widened, and she nodded to the side door. Without a word, she urged him to go.

Chapter Seven

Shelton took several deep breaths as he watched the water cascade into the fountain in the tiny garden behind the church. His heart raced despite his effort to calm it. Oh, shit! Nevil had been right. They shouldn't have come. It had been a tender ceremony, beautiful and yet painful. But it just reinforced his desire for something he'd never have.

He rubbed a hand over his face, smearing a few tears. What made him so stupid about this? It had to be the months they'd been separated. He just needed time to regain his confidence where Nevil was concerned. Nevil didn't need to be his husband for that.

A small pain stabbed his heart, but he ignored it. He had to pull himself together before Nevil came to look for him. He jumped when arms slid unexpectedly around his waist and then leaned back with a sigh against Nevil's hard chest. He laughed when Nevil nuzzled his neck, his lips tickling his skin.

"What are you doing out here?" Nevil asked, his breath warm on Shelton's cheek.

"Jet lag, I guess," Shelton said. He latched onto the first excuse that sprang to mind.

Nevil muttered unintelligible words and planted kisses along Shelton's jaw line. He turned Shelton in his arms and kissed him with a passion he seldom displayed in public. Shelton's hands slid into Nevil's hair and held him in place as he returned the kiss with all the love in his heart.

They were both breathing hard when they separated. A small grin slipped onto Nevil's face, and he touched Shelton's bruised mouth with gentle fingers. "Sorry, didn't mean to do that. But you're so damned delicious."

"You too..."

Heat spread through Shelton as a wicked light appeared in Nevil's beautiful eyes. He pressed Shelton back against the fountain's rim, ground their stiffening cocks together, and laughed when Shelton darted a look over his shoulder. "We still have a few minutes."

Nevil chewed his lips and Shelton wondered at the excitement on his face as Nevil took his hands. "I should go on my knees for this, but that would put me on level with your tempting dick, and I'd forget what I was going to say."

"Nevil!"

Nevil chuckled and then turned Shelton's hands, pressing a kiss to the center of each. He raised his gaze, and Shelton's heart thumped at the emotion that shimmered in the turquoise depths of his eyes. "I love you, Shelton," Nevil told him. He cleared his throat when his voice broke. "Will you marry me?"

Shelton opened his mouth and then closed it. He swallowed and searched Nevil's sober expression. "You're serious..."

"Never more so, love."

"I thought—"

"So did I! But seeing Percy and Brandon just now... Marriage isn't just about you and me. It's sharing our commitment to each other with the world. I like that idea." He pulled Shelton into his arms. "Then everyone will know you're off the market for good."

For an instant, Shelton couldn't speak. He searched his mind, anxious for the right words to say to lighten the mood while tears filled his eyes. He leaned to whisper in Nevil's ear, "Does that mean I get to call you my wife?"

Nevil shouted, and laughter lingered in his voice when he spoke, "Don't you dare! Husband is fine." His face softened. "Husband... Yeah, I can do that," he murmured. He gave Shelton a kiss of love and joy that sealed the bargain.

The door to the church opened behind them, and Shelton pushed Nevil back with a breathless laugh, heart pounding when the marriage party emerged into the garden. The group tossed curious looks their way, and Tera broke off, coming toward them.

"Oh. That's perfect." Shelton swallowed the lump in his throat but couldn't control the wide grin on his face while happiness spilled from his heart.

Nevil squeezed his hand. "Can I tell them?"

Was he kidding? "Absolutely," he said fervently, keeping hold of Nevil's hand as they went to meet their friends.

MERRY

CHRISTMAS,

SHELTON

Chapter One

Shelton snuggled into the soft quilts on the floor, safe and warm while the wind howled against the thick walls of the cabin. A stray gust blew down the chimney, causing the flames to dance and crackle behind the screen. Firelight flickered on the ceiling, and Shelton watched it mingle with the blue and green reflections from the Christmas tree in the corner.

The clock on the mantle chimed midnight, and he smiled. Christmas Eve. Nevil snorted and moved restlessly. Shelton rolled to his side, spooning up against the sleek body that, even after two and a half years together, could drive him crazy with need. Nevil sighed and settled back into sleep, and Shelton nuzzled his neck, pleasantly sore and sated from their earlier lovemaking.

His face heated as he recalled the things Nevil had done with him. Shelton pressed his forehead into Nevil's shoulder blade, slightly embarrassed even though Nevil slept and didn't see him. They'd spent the day cross-country skiing and then returned to the cabin and warmed up in the shower. Afterward, they sat naked on the rug in front of the fireplace and sipped a bottle of wine.

Nevil had stolen a candy cane from the tree. "Dessert," he explained, settling into the quilts with an arm across Shelton's bare shoulders. Shelton watched the red and white stripes disappear between Nevil's perfect lips, and his dick thickened. Nevil caught his rapt gaze, leaned over, and gave him a peppermint kiss.

"Taste?" he asked and held the candy to Shelton's lips. Shelton caught the cane between his teeth, and Nevil gasped slightly as he sucked with purpose on the sweet end. "Oh, lord," Nevil said, sounding breathless, and pushed Shelton down and straddled him. His hard cock pushed against Shelton's stomach when he stretched across him and licked at the cane still caught in his lips.

Removing the candy, Nevil gave him a deep, lingering kiss and then pulled back, a gleam of mischief in his eyes. "I know somewhere else I'd like to stick this," he confessed and gave the candy a provocative lick.

Shelton blinked, though he shouldn't have been surprised by anything Nevil's wicked imagination suggested. "I'm not sure…"

Nevil chuckled, but his voice caressed Shelton's ear when he bent and whispered, "Let me pleasure you, love."

Shelton met his hot gaze, and a shiver of anticipation burned through him. At his nod, Nevil rolled him over and had him kneel with his face pressed into the pillows.

He kneaded Shelton's muscular ass. "So sweet," he murmured and spread Shelton open.

Shelton shivered, moaning as Nevil's warm tongue slid over his sensitive hole and made little darts inside. Shelton's dick lengthened, and he rocked gently, rubbing it against his thighs as Nevil continued to suck at him.

Nevil's wet tongue loosened him up, and then Nevil pushed the slim, hard candy against his hole and nudged it into the tight opening. Shelton pictured how it looked sticking out of his ass and wasn't sure whether he felt aroused or wanted to burst out laughing. "Nevil?"

"Sweets for my sweet," Nevil replied, his voice thick as he slid the candy cane back and forth into him. Nevil licked at the puckered skin clenching the candy, and Shelton trembled, his senses whirling into lust. He wanted to scream for Nevil to fuck him already and slid a hand down to pull at his balls.

"That's it, baby," Nevil said, his voice slurred with need. Nevil plucked the candy from him, and Shelton waited in agony while Nevil reached for the lube on the coffee table. At last, Nevil's thick, amazing cock slid home and filled Shelton's world with ecstasy.

Shelton groaned with the erotic memory and bit his lip, cock stirring. If he didn't hover on the verge of sleep, he'd wake Nevil up for another round. As it was, he'd begun to doze off when Nevil's body jerked in his arms. "What is it, honey?"

Nevil rolled to face him. The fire had died down to coals, but the Christmas lights were enough to see the pain creasing Nevil's forehead. "I don't feel right," he murmured and put his hands on his flat stomach. "I feel achy..." His turquoise eyes widened in the half light. "I think Tera might be having her baby."

Shelton's heart jumped. *Stay calm.* The car was surely snowed in, and if he panicked, Nevil would have them in their snowshoes, hiking to the main lodge over two miles away. Wind shook the windows, reinforcing the need to keep his partner thinking clearly even if it meant playing down the strong bond he knew existed between the siblings. "Honey, I know Tera is your twin and all," he said levelly. "But sympathetic labor pains? Really?"

Nevil frowned, but then a sheepish smile spread over his face. "You're probably right. I just wish we had phone service so I could check on her."

"The people at the lodge said they'd send someone if we got a message. And besides, it was snowing when we got in, and by the sound of that wind, I don't think it's stopped."

"Yeah." Nevil sighed, sounding discouraged.

"Tell you what." Shelton pulled him tight against his side, wishing he could do more. "We'll ski down to the lodge in the morning and call Tera to see what's going on. Deal?"

"I suppose." Nevil didn't sound convinced, but he relaxed into Shelton's arms as another gust of wind swept against the cabin. "Maybe we should have stayed home..."

"Nevil! Tera's the one who sent us away. She's not due for another week and didn't want us hovering."

"True." Nevil gave in and then surprised Shelton by reaching for his left hand. "You're an amazing boyfriend," he said, kissing the fourth finger where a ring should have been this weekend. "You haven't said a word about me postponing our wedding so I could be accessible if Tera needs me."

"That's because I understand. You're going to be an uncle! It's fantastic. And Tera's your sister and has had a difficult pregnancy. Of course you should be here instead of off on our honeymoon, wherever that's going to be.

Besides, I'm excited to see you hold that little person for the first time. It will be incredible."

Nevil turned Shelton's hand and kissed his palm. "I love you," he said and met Shelton's lips in a kiss.

They nestled into the warm quilts and lingered over gentle caresses until Nevil slept again. Shelton watched his face as it relaxed. So beautiful. His heart swelled in his chest; he loved this man so much. He'd panicked a little when Nevil said he wanted to postpone their wedding without setting a future date. At twenty-seven, Nevil was more beautiful than ever with a confidence that drew eyes wherever they went.

Shelton sighed. Nevil had recently been made a partner in his very successful architectural firm, in demand by a more upscale clientele than in the past, while Shelton had once again been passed over for promotion. What did this successful, lovely man need him for? Shelton closed his eyes, hating the jealousy that stung him at times. He wished he had a switch to that particular emotion he could shut off for good. He didn't like that part of himself.

He burrowed against Nevil's warmth, breathed in his scent, and finally slept.

*

Shelton woke from a sound sleep, disoriented by a pounding on the door. Untangling from Nevil, he sat up, heart racing. A glance at the clock showed it was barely five o'clock in the morning. What the hell? The pounding resumed, and he scrambled to his feet, taking a second to slip on sweatpants before unlocking the door. The wind had died down, and Shelton blinked at the snow piled up against the cabin walls. A slight figure huddled on the step, illuminated by the porch light, and without hesitation, Shelton drew him into the warmth of the room, closing the door on the bitter night.

"What's happened?"

Shelton jumped a little at Nevil's voice and blinked in the light that went on overhead. There was a gasp from the bundle under his hand, and he searched the pale face the young man raised. The pretty blue eyes weren't looking at him, and he followed his gaze to where Nevil stood in all his naked splendor. Nevil scowled at their interest and pulled on the cotton pajama bottoms he'd picked up.

Shelton gave the boy a slight shake, knocking snow off his jacket and cap. "God, you're soaked through. You need to get out of these clothes. Nevil, can you stir up the fire?"

"Of course."

As if knowing the danger, the young man stripped off his coat and sopping shirt while Shelton unlaced his boots and carefully slipped them off, leaving the socks for now. Ski pants and Under Armour were lowered, and the man leaned a hand on Shelton's shoulder as he stepped out of them. Shelton glanced up and found himself on eye level with a pair of dark boxers that did little to cover the treasures beneath. His gaze swept up a tight stomach and muscular chest and clashed with laughing eyes. Trouble!

He cleared his throat. "Come to the fire and I'll check for frostbite."

The newcomer followed him, lifting the cap off a shock of copper hair. He sat on the quilts, and Nevil draped another one over his shoulders while Shelton knelt beside him. "Hands first," he said and slid the wet gloves by careful inches off his hands. The skin felt cold and white, but the fingertips weren't blue. "Can you move them?"

He frowned when the young man didn't answer and met his puzzled gaze. "You're really concerned, aren't you?"

The guy sounded slightly amused, and Shelton felt the blush in his cheeks as he answered, "Yes. I saw a boy with frostbite last winter, in Colorado. It was...painful to witness. Let's check those toes."

He removed the damp socks with the same care as the gloves and sighed in relief when the man wiggled each toe.

Nevil snorted from where he leaned against the mantle watching the proceedings. "Now that we know nothing is going to fall off, can you tell us what the hell you're doing here?"

"Tera Shaw left a message for you at the lodge." He smirked when Nevil straightened, tense. "I volunteered to bring it. She says she's fine, but that they're admitting her to the hospital in the morning. She'd like you to be there as soon as you can."

"I'll go immediately."

"No, sir. The snow's not too bad at the lodge, but worse up here. We'll have to wait for the snowplow to get your car out."

Nevil paced the room, cursing under his breath. Shelton heard the young man's breath quicken as he watched the lithe movements of Nevil's sleek body and frowned. "What's your name?" he asked as a distraction.

"Tommy Stephens."

Of course it was. A cute name for a pretty face and sexy, youthful body. Damn.

"Well, Tommy, thanks for risking your neck for us. Why don't you get some sleep here by the fire?" Shelton climbed stiffly to his feet and went to Nevil's side. "Come to bed, honey." Nevil grunted, and Shelton slid an arm around his waist. "Try to sleep, at least a little. It's going to be a long day tomorrow."

Nevil relaxed against him. "You're right." He allowed Shelton to lead him to their room and paused in the doorway to glance back at Tommy. "Thanks, man."

"My pleasure," Tommy said with a purr.

Shelton's lips thinned at the interest in the young man's gaze and tugged Nevil into the room, purposefully closing the door. He pushed Nevil onto the bed, cuddled up to him under the blankets, and held him close until they slept.

Chapter Two

Shelton woke and stared groggily at the dim sunlight peeking through the curtains. His gaze flicked to the clock. Seven? God, he'd hoped to sleep longer. He eased out from under Nevil and slipped on quiet feet from the room. A heap in the quilts by the fire assured him Tommy still slept, and he wrinkled his brow as he headed for the bathroom. It had been brave of the young man to bring them Tera's message. He hoped the snowplow came early so Nevil wouldn't spend the day worrying.

The spray of the shower felt wonderful on his neck and shoulders, and Shelton caught himself dozing off. Wouldn't do to use all the hot water. He soaped up and rinsed when he heard the bathroom door creak open and then close. His heart pounded. Nevil! Maybe it was a weakness, but he'd become a slave to Nevil's desires and a very willing one at that. He took a minute to enjoy the slide of soap over his growing dick and then washed the suds off his balls and turned off the water.

Smiling with anticipation, he slid open the shower door and blinked at the redhead standing naked by the sink. It took a second for his numbed brain to react. "Oh, sorry. I thought..." Shelton reached for the towel on the hook, his heart pounding as he tried to keep his eyes from Tommy's sleek, hard erection arching toward him.

Tommy's affectionate laugh made him shiver. The young man stepped closer, his pretty blue eyes raking over Shelton. They widened when they reached his scarred dick. "Oh, God," he murmured and touched Shelton, making him jump as his thumb grazed over the rough skin. "I'd love to have this rammed up inside me. Will you fuck me, hon?"

Shelton flushed with heat but controlled his reactions to the blatant invitation. "What are you doing?"

He saw confusion in the lovely eyes, and then Tommy gave him a searching look. A blush stained his white skin, and he stepped back. "Um...sorry. Hands off, huh?"

"Yes, now if you'll get out..."

Tommy threw his hands in the air. "Don't have to ask twice. Really, I'm sorry, man. Thought we could have a little fun. Guess I read you wrong."

Shelton choked on a burst of lust Tommy's words set off and couldn't answer. Instead, he threw the towel over his head and rubbed his wet hair. He sagged against the wall when the door clicked shut. Jesus fuck! That had been harder to do than it should have been. But Tommy had been so vibrant, alive, and hard. He groaned and reached for his aching cock.

Keeping his mind blank, Shelton concentrated on the feel of his hand sliding over skin, squeezing and kneading. Making little grunts of pleasure, he reached lower and rolled his balls together, tugging gently, then rougher. Heat pooled in his stomach, and he returned to his dick. Tingles of bliss raced along his nerves, scorching his blood as he stroked his hard member. So close.

He nearly screamed when the door flung open with a bang, and he let go of his cock with a frustrated moan. Nevil's laugh sent his pulse soaring. "Shelton! You should have woken me up, silly man."

Before Shelton could reply, warm, familiar lips wrapped around his dick and sucked him into the heat he lived for. He didn't even try to hold back as he slid to the back of Nevil's throat and Nevil swallowed him down. Two, three small thrusts, and he came with a cry of joy. This was where he belonged.

Nevil licked him clean, then rose to his feet and lifted the towel from Shelton's head. Shelton blinked at his dazzling smile and then grabbed the back of his head and kissed him with all the passion in his heart.

Nevil eased him back. "What is it, love?"

Shelton shook his head. "Doesn't matter. I love you."

"I love you too." Nevil touched Shelton's wet curls. "I'm taking the snowshoes and hiking back to the lodge with Tommy. Will you wait for the snowplow and bring the car down when the road's clear? I'd like to start home as soon as possible."

"Of course. Be careful, okay?"

Nevil gave him a fond look. "Always! See you soon."

Shelton gazed thoughtfully at the closed door after Nevil left him with one last kiss. It didn't surprise him Nevil wanted to go. He was an experienced hiker, so Shelton didn't worry about his safety. He just wished he hadn't gone with that cute red-headed devil. He smiled wryly. Nevil could hold his own with anyone; Shelton had no doubt about that. He trusted Nevil, and his little prick of jealousy could go fuck itself.

He pulled on his clothes, went into the main part of the cabin, and smiled in surprise. Expecting a mess, it was nice to find the quilts folded into a neat pile and the washed dishes drying on the counter. Maybe the imp would turn out to be not such a bad guy after all. With his mood lightened, Shelton whistled as he set about packing his and Nevil's suitcases and emptying the refrigerator into the cooler. He straightened the cabin, saving the Christmas tree for last.

Shelton sighed a little as he knelt by the tree and gathered the tiny, brightly wrapped boxes together, hoping to God everything was all right with Nevil's delightful twin. He couldn't help wishing he was the one at Nevil's side right now, trudging through the snow instead of being left behind with the packing. It was frustrating when he wanted to be with the ones he loved, doing something.

A rumble disturbed the silence of the cabin, and Shelton went to the door in time to see the snowplow clear the road and start back downhill. Perfect! Now to dig out the car...

It took little over an hour to clear the drift of snow from the Prius so he could back it into the road. He packed the trunk and backseat with their belongings and then locked up the cabin and started down the mountainside in low gear. They'd put chains on the tires yesterday, but Shelton still slid a few times on hidden ice before the rustic building came into view.

It proved hard to find an open spot in the crowded lot of the ski lodge, but finally, Shelton parked and hurried inside. He'd hoped to find Nevil in the lobby. When he saw no sign of him or the beautiful redhead, he went to the information counter and introduced himself. "Is there a message for me?"

"Let me check. Shelton, is it? Yes, here you go, sir."

Shelton smiled as the young woman handed him an envelope with a flourish. He always found the staff at Sugarpine Lodge to be amazingly friendly and helpful. It was why he and Nevil skied there rather than other popular resorts.

His hands shook as he opened the note, and his smile dimmed while he read Nevil's scrawled message. "You left without me?" he whispered, slightly hurt, though not surprised. He'd suspected Nevil wouldn't lose a minute getting to Tera's side. But to accept the offer of a lift from Tommy? Damn. Shelton hoped he wouldn't have to slap that pretty redhead's face when they met again. If Nevil hadn't smacked him first. Nevil's patience only stretched so far.

He bought coffee and a sandwich for the road and then returned to the car and started down the mountain. His knuckled whitened on the slippery road over the pass, but once on the other side, the road cleared of any lingering ice, and he could settle into the two-hour drive to Portland.

Shelton ate his sandwich, sipped his coffee, and hummed along to his music to pass the time. Worry crept into his thoughts as he neared the busy downtown area of the city. God, he hoped he found everything okay with Tera. Rain pounded against the hood of the Prius. Once at the hospital, Shelton parked in the first lot he came to and dashed for the nearest entrance to the birthing center.

Collecting Tera's room number at the front counter, he hurried to the elevators. The ride up seemed interminable, and Shelton's pulse quickened as he followed the long hallway to Tera's room. Robert rose from a chair by the bed as he entered, putting a finger to his lips for silence. "Tera's finally asleep," he whispered.

"Still pregnant?" Shelton asked, peering around Tera's husband to see her.

"The baby's in a little distress so they're keeping Tera here overnight. If things don't improve, they'll do a C-section in the morning."

Shelton gnawed a lip. "Is there any danger?"

"No more than usual with this procedure. We just want Tera and the baby to be healthy."

"Of course." Shelton gripped Robert's hand. "This is good news. Nevil was worried sick. Um... where is he?"

"He mentioned getting a drink at that Irish pub down the street and waiting for you before going home. There shouldn't be any excitement around here until tomorrow."

Shelton nodded and then gestured toward the bed, tiptoeing over when Robert smiled. Tera looked tired but beautiful against the white pillowcases. Delight filled Shelton, knowing she was in good hands and that they should be holding her baby this time tomorrow.

"Make sure to call us if there's any change," he told Robert as he made to leave.

"Will do. Make sure Nevil sleeps. He looked pretty done in when I saw him."

"Thanks, Robert. We'll see you in the morning." Shelton waved and then made his way back through the labyrinth of hallways and outside to gather the car and find Nevil.

Chapter Three

Nevil stared into the amber liquid of his drink and then took a sip of the warm beer and made a face. He glanced at his watch for the hundredth time. Where the hell was Shelton? And goddamn! He wished that woman would quit screeching. Her singing shrilled like a banshee with a toothache.

He straightened on the stool. Okay, he was tired and pissy. Tommy squirmed on the barstool next to him, and Nevil glowered. That little piece of candy fluff hadn't helped his mood either. Sure, he at least owed him a meal for the ride down, but he wished the guy would finish and go.

They'd stopped at a gas station at the bottom of the mountain, and Nevil had gone into the lavatory to wash the tiredness from his face. He'd smiled as he fished his dick out at the urinal, remembering walking in on Shelton that morning. Fuck! That had been hot. Shelton standing, knees slightly bent, towel draped over his head so only his lower half showed as his hand pumped that amazing cock of his.

Nevil had moaned, his dick thickening as he recalled Shelton's rough shaft sliding between his lips to lodge in his throat. Hot, tangy come filled his mouth, coating his throat so he had to swallow or choke. Moving his hips, Nevil lazily fucked his fist as he imagined bending Shelton over the sink and driving into his sweet ass. He didn't realize he wasn't alone until a body plastered against his back and a hand reached round to close over his. "Need help?"

Tommy's thick cock nudged against his ass while talented fingers ran over his hardness. Shit! That felt good.

A few years ago, he would have had a divine ten minutes with this sexy little prick. But all he could think of now was the hurt it would bring to Shelton's eyes, and no way would he do that.

"Do you mind?" he snarled and shoved his shoulder against Tommy.

Tommy grunted and stumbled back, sounding surprised. "Okay! Sorry. Thought you could use a little fun."

"Not with you." Nevil, purposefully blunt, buttoned his fly and stomped from the dank room.

Tommy's offer had been more tempting than he cared to admit. They hardly spoke for the rest of the drive into Portland, and Nevil began to wish he'd waited for Shelton at the lodge after all as Tommy ate his hamburger with agonizing slowness.

Movement at the entranceway made Nevil glance across the pub, and he spotted Shelton hesitating in the doorway. He took a deep breath, his worries melting away when Shelton saw him and grinned. The smile slipped as Shelton's gaze shifted to Tommy. A strange expression flickered across his face, but it disappeared as he crossed the room and walked straight into Nevil's open arms.

They didn't speak for a moment and then Shelton stepped back, a blush on his face. Adorable. Nevil touched his hot cheek and played with a chestnut curl brushing his chin. "I see you made it off the mountain safely."

"You too. Thanks, Tommy."

The redhead flicked him a glance and winked. "No problem. Anytime."

Shelton raised a brow when he turned abruptly back to his plate, but Nevil shook his head. "Never mind him. Come on." He took Shelton's elbow and guided him from the noisy pub.

"The car's this way." Shelton motioned up the street when Nevil started in the opposite direction.

"I want to do something first," he said enigmatically and chuckled under his breath when Shelton looked ready to rebel. "It'll only take a minute. Promise."

He took Shelton's hand as they walked along the sidewalk and then pulled him into the gay bar on the corner. The club had begun to fill for happy hour, but Nevil found a secluded corner and took Shelton in his arms. Slow, sultry music played over the speakers. Nevil's hands slid down Shelton's back to his ass and nudged him closer. Shelton resisted and then sighed and relaxed into Nevil's embrace. Being slightly shorter, his cock and balls fit deliciously against Nevil's. Perfect.

Shelton's arms slid around his neck, and Nevil held him close as they swayed in time to the music. He couldn't remember the last time they had danced together, and Nevil took full advantage of it as he breathed in Shelton's subtle cologne and hint of sweat. He gloried in the feel of Shelton's strong body pressed against his, their cocks crushed together. Nevil ground against him, and he heard Shelton's soft moan and felt the tremor that ran through him.

Sliding a finger under his chin, he tilted Shelton's face up and gasped at the love and desire warming his hazel eyes.

"I love you," he murmured and grazed Shelton's lips with his own. He caught Shelton's groan in a kiss, plundering his sweet mouth until his head reeled. He forgot where he was and slid his hand down the back of Shelton's jeans, stroking the crack of his delectable ass.

"Take me home?"

Nevil gloried at the pleading note in Shelton's voice. God, he loved this man!

"If you want," he teased and blinked in surprise at the dark flush that swept Shelton's face. "What is it?"

Shelton avoided his gaze. "Nothing. Let's go."

"Not until you tell me what's wrong." He watched with some concern as emotions chased across his features. "Shelton?"

"Fuck, Nevil. I didn't want to have to tell you. It's so stupid."

"Tell me anyway."

Shelton moved back from him, looking miserable. "I was jealous when I saw Tommy with you at the pub. And now you don't seem to want to take me—"

Nevil stopped his words with a hard kiss and shook him slightly. "Don't be absurd. How could that little prick mean anything to me?"

"I know! But there's this niggling voice in my head that I don't know how to shut up. And it has a point, Nevil. I bet every man in this room wishes he was with you."

Nevil chuckled, amused, though also flattered that Shelton would think so. "There's only one problem with that thought, love," he whispered in Shelton's ear. "They're not looking at me. They're looking at you."

"Ha!"

Nevil took Shelton's shoulders and turned him to face the room. He delighted in Shelton's snort and the laughter in his voice. "They don't count. Jesus, Nevil."

Shelton left his arms, and Nevil followed him toward the boisterous group at the bar, admiring his casual sexiness in loose jeans and sweater. If nothing else, his man knew how to dress.

The nearest man stood and pulled Shelton against his side. "There's our pretty boy. Wondered if you two would stop molesting each other and come say hi."

Nevil grunted. Leave it to Michael Barns to get his pets in first. He stood back while Shelton got a round of kisses from everyone and raised a hand to the lovely brunet on the end. "Hey, Brandon. Where's Percy?"

"Kicked me out of the house. Not like that!" he rushed to say at a united gasp. "He hinted he has something special planned for Christmas Eve, and I can't come home until seven. So, are you an uncle yet?"

"Not yet." Nevil tugged Shelton out of reach of Michael's wandering fingers and placed a hand firmly on the small of his back before continuing. "But I will be this time tomorrow, one way or another."

"Oh, that's great! Congratulations. Give Tera and Robert a hug from us."

"Definitely."

He glanced over as the door to the club opened with a gust of cool air, and a burst of mischief took hold of him when he heard Michael's indrawn breath behind him. Tommy Stephen's ginger locks fairly glowed in the pulsing light of the bar, bewitching around his pale features.

"Hey, Tommy!" Nevil waved him over.

Tommy looked startled, and then a smile touched his full lips and he swayed as he approached the group of men. Nevil chuckled, and Shelton flashed him a look, his own eyes dancing with laughter. Their friends wouldn't know what hit them!

Nevil took Tommy's arm when he came up. "Tommy, meet the gang."

Michael stood immediately, a gleam of definite interest in his green eyes. "I'm Michael. Here, take my spot. Glen!" he called the bartender. "A drink for this lovely man, please."

Nevil laughed out loud as Tommy simpered and climbed up on the stool Michael held out for him. He leaned over to Brandon as the others crowded around the pretty newcomer. "Go home, love. This is no place for a happily married man."

"Sound advice." Brandon tossed some money on the bar and followed them out of the club. They parted at the sidewalk, and Brandon embraced them. "I'm off to do some shopping. Merry Christmas."

"Same to you. Give Percy our love," Shelton told him.

Nevil seconded him and then touched Shelton's arm as Brandon made for his car across the street. "Want to walk a little?" Night had come early, and the trees looked beautiful in their Christmas glory.

They linked arms and headed downtown. Soon, Nevil slipped his arm across Shelton's shoulders, and he tilted his face up for Nevil's kiss. He blinked as a fat raindrop splashed on his cheek, and Nevil frowned. "Warm enough? We should have gotten your jacket and hat from the car."

"I'm fine," Shelton protested. "Hey, they have the tree lit."

His cheer was contagious, and Nevil's heart gave a funny little skip, filling him with warmth for the precious man with him. Shelton pulled him into the town square and halted at the foot of the tree, the Christmas lights washing over him. Nevil stood behind him, pulled Shelton back against his chest, and wrapped him in his arms.

Shelton gave a contented sigh. "Just beautiful."

"Yes, you are."

Nevil knew it was the corniest thing he could say, but the words had simply slipped out. He grazed Shelton's blushing, smiling face with a kiss. "Do you know how much I love you?" he asked gruffly.

Shelton turned in his arms to meet his gaze. "I'm not sure. Maybe you need to show me."

Nevil's cock jumped at the invitation. "I could eat you alive," he growled in Shelton's ear and stole a sweet kiss, wanting a thousand more. He pulled back when a young couple brushed by them, laughing and chatting. They cooed to the baby in the woman's arms, and then the man stepped away and pulled a camera out of his pocket.

"Can I help?" Nevil offered and held out his hand.

"That would be great. Thanks."

The young man handed over his tiny camera and joined his wife under the brilliantly lit tree. Nevil snapped a few pictures, and then the couple joined them. For some reason, the young mother handed the squirming bundle to Shelton, who gazed at the child with wondering eyes. "She's so tiny!"

"Yes, she is, but growing every day." The man turned to Nevil. "I'm Tony, by the way. This is my wife, Angie, and baby, Tina."

"I'm Nevil, and this charming man is my partner, Shelton."

Shelton flashed them a smile and then turned his attention back to the tiny girl. Nevil watched the side of Shelton's face. He sensed Shelton's disappointment with his use of the term 'partner' when they were to have been married by this time if things had gone differently. He smiled, thinking with excitement of a certain Christmas gift he had for Shelton. Now to get Shelton home so he could open it.

"Give the baby back, hon," he teased. "We'll have one of those adorable creatures of our own tomorrow."

"You're having a baby?" Angie asked in delight. "Adopting?"

Nevil gave the couple a close look but saw only a friendly curiosity in their expressions. Shelton spoke before he could answer. "Nevil's twin is having her baby tomorrow, if all goes well."

"Congratulations! On Christmas, huh?"

"Tell me about it." Nevil rolled his eyes. "I can already tell the kid's going to break my bank account."

They said goodbye over a shared laugh. Thinking of Tera, Nevil experienced a strange fluttering in his stomach.

It didn't hurt, more of a feeling of pressure.

Shelton touched his hand, and the twinge vanished. "Baby pains?"

Nevil felt the tingle of a blush and then realized Shelton looked genuinely concerned. "Maybe, but nothing serious. Strange, huh?"

Shelton shrugged. "You and Tera are close. I'm not surprised by anything between you two."

He sounded distracted and Nevil followed his gaze across the square. A young man sat on the bottom steps, head bowed as if exhausted or discouraged. He shivered in a wet T-shirt and jeans and clutched a foam cup as if his life depended on the dark liquid inside.

Nevil slipped an arm around him. "What are you thinking?"

"He doesn't look more than nineteen or twenty."

"If that."

"Damn, Nevil, it's Christmas Eve. Why is he alone like this?"

Nevil kissed his cheek. "He's not a puppy we can take home."

Shelton grunted and broke away from him, and Nevil followed him across the square. They looked down at the young man a moment, but he ignored them, eyes on his battered shoes. With a quick movement, Shelton pulled his bulky sweater over his head, leaving on the turtleneck. He folded it and put it on the step beside the man who at last raised his face, thin and pale, with wide bewildered blue eyes.

Nevil bent close and said gently, "The rescue mission is up the street. You can get a meal and bed for the night. Go on."

The young man dropped his gaze back to the cement under his shoes. Nevil tugged on Shelton's sleeve, holding him against his side as they returned to the sidewalk and headed for the car. "It's getting chilly. Let's get you home, love."

"Think he'll go?"

"Maybe. Probably." They glanced back and watched the young man pull the sweater over his head. "At least he'll be warm." He kissed Shelton's sad eyes, then hurried him down the street.

As they approached the Prius, he fished the keys from a pocket to let Shelton in and then slid into the driver's seat and quickly started the engine to get the heater going. He set the volume low on the Christmas music he'd downloaded last month and pulled carefully into traffic. The streets glittered with lights and last-minute shoppers. Shelton smiled at a Santa on a corner handing out candy canes, and Nevil let out a relieved breath. Shelton had a very tender heart.

"Did you remember to get the gifts from under the tree?" he asked by way of a distraction.

"First thing! I wasn't about to leave those behind."

"Greedy," Nevil teased and put his hand on Shelton's thigh, guiding the car with his left hand. After a moment,

Shelton laced his fingers through Nevil's and picked up his hand. He kissed each knuckle and then slipped a finger between his lips. Nevil groaned at the wet, warm suction on his digit.

"Not fair," he panted. His dick pressed uncomfortably against his jeans.

Shelton laughed and let his hand go and immediately placed his in Nevil's lap. He stroked fingers over the bulge there, making Nevil squirm. "Can I help you with that?"

"Sure, if you want us in a ditch. Otherwise, wait till we get home, bad boy."

Still laughing, Shelton leaned his head against the seat cushion. Nevil glanced at him and thought about how beautiful he looked with the holiday lights washing over him. He faced forward and had a hard time concentrating on the road while images of all the naughty things he wanted to do with Shelton played in his mind. He heard Shelton's quickly drawn breath, and his dick swelled as he realized Shelton had some wicked thoughts of his own. *Merry Christmas!*

Chapter Four

Shelton's heart sped up as Nevil turned the car onto their street and parked in the driveway of the brownstone. He'd been touched by the young man's loneliness in the city square and wanted to show Nevil how grateful he was to have him in his life.

When the Prius came to a stop, Nevil turned off the engine, and they hopped out. With unspoken consent, they unpacked the car and hurried into the comfort of home. Shelton carried the box of gifts to the tree while Nevil took the cooler of food to the kitchen and unloaded it into the refrigerator. Shelton turned off the overhead lights so that only the blue and green radiance of the Christmas tree in the corner lit the room. He nibbled his lips as he placed the cheery packages under the tree, wondering what Nevil would think of some of his.

Nevil joined him, sitting on the soft rug and pulling Shelton into his arms. "Hey."

"Hey yourself," Shelton countered and kissed the soft lips he could never get enough of. He groaned when Nevil's tongue slid over his and started a fire along his nerves. He tried to push Nevil back on the rug but Nevil halted him with a hand on his chest. He glanced up to see Nevil's eyes dancing with glee.

"Presents first, my love! I've been waiting all day," Nevil told him and snatched a box from the bright pile before Shelton could say anything. Shelton watched his face as he opened the box and saw his eyes widen. Nevil made a surprised sound and lifted the hot pink, padded handcuffs from the package. "Oh my." He looked at Shelton and winked. "Is someone being naughty?"

Shelton's face heated. "Well, we had the weekend at the cabin, and I thought... Maybe we could experiment..." His words came to a stumbling halt, and he blushed furiously when Nevil chuckled.

Nevil ran kisses over his face, and Shelton allowed himself to be lowered down onto the rug. He arched his hips when Nevil straddled him, so their cocks ground together. "Oh, definitely naughty." Nevil purred and clasped one of the cuffs around Shelton's wrist.

"I wanted to—"

"Me first," Nevil interrupted. He snaked the other cuff around the claw foot of the couch and fastened Shelton's free wrist. "I think my bad boy needs a little attention."

Shelton collapsed on the rug, curious and intensely aroused, wondering what Nevil had in mind. Nevil reached across him and picked another present.

"Let's see what else you dreamed of," he said and tore off the glittery wrap. He shouted in delight and lifted out the string of anal beads. "Ho ho!" He sent Shelton a smoldering look. "You do remember that Santa is watching, my naughty man?"

"He can join us," Shelton whispered, his mouth going dry at the flash of lust in Nevil's blue-green gaze.

Nevil sputtered. "Fuck, no. I'm not sharing you with some well-endowed elf bearing gifts. Now, what to do with these?" He ran the thick black beads over Shelton's lips, making him shiver. Nevil set them aside and took one of the smaller boxes.

"When do I get my presents?" Shelton protested.

Nevil rocked against him, and Shelton groaned with pleasure at the friction on his dick. "You'll get yours, love. No fear of that!" Nevil pulled the top off the box and then stared in surprise. Giving a muttered oath, he dropped the contents on Shelton's chest. "Expecting someone?"

Shelton's heart lurched. Being in a committed relationship, they hadn't used condoms in years. He'd bought them on a whim, but angry sex with Nevil wasn't what he'd planned. He cursed his fair skin, knowing his face turned red and blotchy from his blushes. "They glow in the dark. I thought it would be fun to hide...and..."

His words trailed off. He couldn't cover his face so he closed his eyes, feeling like a total fool. "Let me up," he said, deeply embarrassed. He wished he'd kept his little fantasies locked inside where they couldn't hurt him.

"No."

He shrugged, unable to speak, and his chest rose and fell with his quick breaths. He turned his face aside when Nevil stretched across him, but Nevil trailed kisses over his hot cheek and nuzzled his neck.

"I adore you, you know that?" Nevil murmured and nibbled Shelton's earlobe, sending shivers through him. "I love that you want to play with me. Shelton, look at me. I have to confess, and I want to see your eyes when I do it."

Shelton opened his eyes and met Nevil's earnest gaze. Nevil took a breath. "Tommy came on to me today. Of course I told him to fuck himself, but then I thought he might have done the same to you. When I saw the condoms, I thought he had and that you liked it. That you wanted to have someone besides me too."

"God, Nevil. Why would you think that? You know you have my heart."

Color tinged Nevil's cheeks, and Shelton's heart thudded. Nevil never blushed. There was a hint of shame in his voice when he continued, "Because, my love, for just the briefest second this afternoon, I wanted him back. Less than a heartbeat! Then I thought of you, and all desire for the little shit vanished. You're the only one I want in my arms, ever. Will you forgive me, darling?"

Shelton's emotions felt slightly battered, but Nevil loved and wanted him, and in the end, that was all that mattered. A slow grin spread across his face. "I'm not sure. I think you'll have to make it up to me," he said and thrust his hips to grind his dick against Nevil's.

Joy and mischief glittered in Nevil's eyes. "Really? And how exactly should I do that? Let's see. Handcuffs, check. Anal beads, check. Condoms? We'll save those for later." He tossed them under the tree. He eyed the boxes left over.

"Any more surprises I should know about?"

"Not of this nature," Shelton said, his tone serious.

Nevil shouted. "Right! First thing, remove victim's clothing."

"I'm not—"

"Hush. Here, bite on these." Nevil put the dark beads against Shelton's lips until he opened his mouth and licked along their length. Nevil caught his breath and rolled off him, stretching out on the rug. "Wider?" he asked and slid the smaller end of the link between his lips. Shelton sucked in a few more of the smooth plastic balls, and Nevil moved them gently in and out of his mouth, looking mesmerized. "Good lord," he whispered shakily.

Nevil removed the beads and kissed him, a deep sensual meeting of lips and tongues that sparked desire through Shelton to the tips of his toes and back up to his prick straining against his jeans. Nevil shoved up Shelton's shirt and rubbed his nipples between thumb and fingers, pinching lightly. He lowered his head and bit and licked at them until Shelton tossed his head at the ripples of pleasure.

"Nevil..." He whimpered for more, and Nevil slid his hands down his chest and stomach, his skillful tongue following. Shelton panted as Nevil undid the buttons on his jeans one at a time. Warm lips clamped on the head of his dick, and he cried out as Nevil's tongue darted into the slit, making him crazy with need. Shelton pushed into his mouth, but Nevil drew away and sat back on his heels. Standing smoothly, he stripped out of his clothing, his thick cock bouncing against his flat stomach as he slid off his pants.

Nevil quickly retrieved the lube from the coffee table drawer and then knelt beside Shelton and picked up the beads. There was a gleam in his eyes as they raked over Shelton's prone body that made him tremble. "You know, sweetheart, I think you're too sweet to watch this," Nevil told him and lifted his shirt over his arms, covering his head and plunging him into darkness.

"Nevil!"

"Quiet. Don't make me spank you."

Shelton choked on a laugh that turned into a gasp when Nevil bit his right nipple, then soothed it with his tongue. Nevil tugged Shelton's jeans down and helped him squirm out of them.

"Bend your knees, sweetheart," Nevil instructed.

Shelton pulled his feet up, and Nevil nudged his legs wide apart. He waited, straining to hear any sound from Nevil to let him know what to expect. Nevil licked his dick with his warm tongue, and he jumped, his bones melting at Nevil's wicked chuckle. Oh God! Nevil was capable of anything in this mood.

He heard the squirt of lube and moaned as a slick finger massaged the sensitive skin of his hole. Pressure and then a fat thumb nudged inside him. He winced at the quick pain, but it disappeared as Nevil slid in farther and stroked the walls of his hole, moving in circles to stretch him open.

Nevil removed his thumb. *Here it comes.* A finger slid in, coupled with the first of the rounded beads. Shelton grunted. They didn't hurt but felt foreign, different, decadent. Nevil used his finger to loosen him more, and Shelton groaned as a larger bead eased inside his slick hole. He stifled a cry as two more quickly followed, each striking his prostate as it passed over.

"God, Nevil," he managed to gasp. "I don't know—"

Nevil pulled out his finger, and Shelton choked, a deep moan rising from his chest as the last, largest beads pushed relentlessly in, stretching and filling him. So good. Nothing like the heat and life of Nevil's cock, but then

Nevil made quick little thrusts back and forth with the beads, and his head swam with pleasure.

Straddling him again, Nevil stretched across Shelton's body and pulled his shirt from his face. He sighed as cool air dried the sweat on his forehead.

"Doing okay?" Nevil asked, and Shelton nodded. One of the beads seemed to sit directly on his prostate, and if he clenched his muscles... Nevil reached back and tugged on the ring at the end of the beads, and sparks went off behind Shelton's eyes.

"Shit," he moaned and took a second to catch his breath.

Nevil searched his face. "Tell me, love. Did Tommy solicit you today? I want the truth."

Shelton sighed, knowing his blush gave him away. "Does it matter? I said no."

Nevil touched Shelton's dick. "What did he say? Did he want you to blow him? Did he want to suck you?" He drew an outraged breath when Shelton shrugged. "He wanted to fuck you? Bastard!"

"No, Nevil, it wasn't that."

"Oh." Nevil stroked him. "He wanted this amazing cock inside him. I can understand that."

If anything, Shelton's face flushed hotter. So not attractive. "Please, Nevil, I've forgotten all about him. Can't you?"

"Of course. I'm just a jealous prick. But Shelton, he's given me a great idea. Will you fuck me, love?"

Shelton sucked in a breath. The thought of the anal beads shoved up his ass while Nevil rode his cock sent a jolt of lust straight to his dick. It jumped in Nevil's hand, and Nevil laughed out loud.

"I'll take that as a yes," Nevil murmured and reached for the lube. He frowned at the half empty tube. "This would be easier if you had hands. Oh well, I'll do it myself."

Shelton watched raptly as Nevil squeezed some lube onto his thumb, then reached around and wiggled it into his hole. "Mmm…"

Mesmerized, Shelton looked down his chest at Nevil's beautiful cock rubbing against him as Nevil shoved a finger in to join his thumb. "Nevil…" he began and licked dry lips.

"Shelton?"

"Can I suck on you?" he asked, voice husky with lust as he stared at the glitter of precome on the tip of Nevil's thick cock.

"Hell yes." Nevil moved forward and rubbed the tip of his dick across Shelton's lips. Shelton lapped at it with his tongue, loving the tang and taste of his lover. He opened his mouth, and Nevil slid in, allowing Shelton to take as much as he wanted. Nevil continued to plunge his fingers in his hole, and Shelton sucked him to the back of his throat, swallowing him down.

"Fuck, I'm close," Nevil warned.

Shelton immediately let him go. Nevil pulled his fingers out and squirmed backwards until Shelton's dick pressed against him. He pushed down, and Shelton groaned as the hot walls of his hole closed around him. Nevil pulled up, and the force of his push downwards shoved the anal beads deeper into Shelton's ass.

"God," he panted. Nevil rocked on him, each movement striking a bead against his prostate. His orgasm started as a burn along his nerves, bliss racing downwards to gather in his balls. He tried to speak and strangled on a moan, but Nevil knew. He pulled on his own cock and shouted as he came in a stream of semen up Shelton's chest to his chin. His muscles convulsed around Shelton, and Shelton let go, shooting his come deep in Nevil's hot ass.

Nevil collapsed against him as they caught their breaths and then lovingly licked the come off Shelton's chin and shared it in a kiss. Shelton's heart swelled as he tasted Nevil. "I love you."

"Me too." Nevil reached up and undid the cuffs from Shelton's wrists. As Shelton rubbed circulation into his arms, Nevil gently pulled out the anal beads, making him shudder with one last burst of pleasure. They snuggled under the tree, exchanging sweet kisses.

Chapter Five

After a few pleasant minutes, Nevil leaned on an elbow. "Will you open a gift for me? I've been waiting weeks to see your reaction."

"I don't think I can take very many more gifts," Shelton countered with a smile as he sat up and leaned against the couch.

"You'll like this one," Nevil promised. They cleaned up with Nevil's shirt, then Nevil knelt by the tree to retrieve the present. Shelton admired his toned body bathed in the blue and green Christmas lights.

It surprised him when Nevil hesitated to hand him the bright gift bag. "I hope you like it," he said, his voice anxious.

"I'm sure I will, honey," Shelton told him, wondering what it was all about. Untying the sparkling ribbon on the bag, he found a small box wrapped in tissue with a note attached.

"Open it," Nevil urged with suppressed excitement.

Shelton set the note aside and undid the tissue, lifted the lid on the box. Gold gleamed in the soft light, and Shelton's hands shook as he raised his gaze to Nevil's.

"What does this mean?"

"Read the note!"

Shelton fumbled with the paper, and he blinked, eyes filled with tears as he read the scrawled words. Nevil cupped his face with a gentle hand, his gaze warm. "Will you marry me, love? The soonest I could set everything up is early June."

"Yes," Shelton breathed and couldn't continue. He touched the gold wedding bands that somehow made it all real.

Nevil laughed, though his voice held a hint of tears when he spoke. "It's settled then." He couldn't stifle a yawn. "Okay, I need a nap before we continue celebrating." He stood and held a hand out to Shelton. "We'll finish the gifts later. Coming?"

"Definitely." Shelton set the rings and note on the mantle and followed Nevil to their room.

Slipping under the blankets, Nevil pulled Shelton into his arms and kissed the tears off his face. "Merry Christmas, love."

"Merry Christmas, Nevil. I love you."

*

Shelton woke abruptly, still groggy as he reached for Nevil. "Darling?"

"Oh, God." Nevil curled into a ball on the bed, and Shelton rubbed his back, his heart pounding.

"Is it Tera?"

"Yeah." Nevil gasped and then gave a sudden laugh. "Oh lord! How do women do this? Tera's fine. Happy. She's having the baby now, though."

"Okay." Shelton kicked off the covers and rolled to his feet.

Nevil climbed out the other side of the bed, and they dressed, chatting like mad in their excitement. Shelton's heart spilled over with happiness for Nevil, knowing he had looked forward to this day for several years. He might never have a child of his own, but being an uncle would be the next best thing.

They hurried from the apartment, Nevil dropping his keys several times before Shelton held out his hand. "I'll drive."

He threaded through the sparse traffic across town and found a parking spot close to the doors of the birthing center. Nevil jumped from the car and sprinted across the lot. Shelton chuckled, locked the doors, and followed his delightful partner. Nevil's love for his twin had always warmed his heart.

Nevil disappeared through the doors, but Shelton was quick to follow, making his way to the birthing center. Tera's room seemed spacious and comfortable, but at the moment, crowded with nurses and the doctor, the air was charged with tension and excitement. Nevil motioned to him from the corner, and Shelton hurried to his side, lacing their fingers together.

"Little Sarah's coming," Nevil told him, his eyes trained on the tableau at the bed. Tera cried out in pain, and Shelton slipped his arms around Nevil when he jerked as if struck.

"She'll be all right," he murmured and pulled Nevil's head down to his shoulder to stroke his hair. He felt the tremors running through his body as Tera's moans increased. "Do you want to wait outside?"

"No. I'm okay," Nevil whispered. "I don't like to hear her hurting, that's all."

"Poor Robert looks ready to faint," Shelton told him, and Nevil laughed slightly.

"Don't blame him…" Nevil's voice trailed off as the doctor gave quick instructions. There was a flurry of activity, one last sharp moan, and then the cries of a baby filled the room.

"Thank god." Nevil drew in a deep breath as cheers went up around them. He raised his face, and Shelton brushed his tears away with a gentle thumb.

"Congratulations, Uncle Nevil," he teased.

Nevil gave him a quick kiss and then rocked on his heels as they waited for the nurses to finish their duties and hand a wailing Sarah to her mother's arms. They went over to the bed, and Nevil embraced his twin, baby and all.

"I'm so proud of you, honey," he murmured, and Shelton heard the emotion in his voice. Shelton's throat tightened with joy for him as Nevil leaned close and gave the tiny red cheek a gentle kiss. "Welcome to the world, Sarah Marie. I've waited a long time to see you."

He jumped back when Sarah wailed, sounding angry and frustrated.

"Our little girl's hungry," Tera murmured indulgently. "Robert, will you help?"

"Here, little one." Robert took the squirming bundle in the crook of his arm while Nevil helped Tera sit up. A pillow slipped, and Robert turned to Shelton. "You're up, Uncle Shelton," he said, and Shelton hastily took Sarah while Robert arranged pillows to Tera's liking.

He stared, fascinated, into the little red face on his arm, cooing and rocking until the loud wails quieted. He felt inordinately proud when Sarah stopped crying, her face scrunched and unhappy. Nevil gathered him into an embrace, Sarah between them.

"You're a natural," Nevil told him. Shelton looked up, but Nevil focused on the baby. He touched a wrinkled cheek, and awe hushed his voice when he spoke. "Absolutely amazing." Nevil's happy gaze swept to him, his face wreathed in smiles.

Shelton placed a kiss beside his mouth. "Merry Christmas, Nevil."

"Merry Christmas, Shelton," Nevil murmured and gave him a kiss full of promise.

Epilogue

Shelton leaned his head back on the side of the hot tub, letting the mountain air cool the heat in his cheeks. A sprinkle of stars dotted the indigo sky, and he sighed inwardly at their beauty. Nevil and he usually came to Sugarpine Lodge in winter to ski, but springtime appeared to be nice there as well. Nevil took the seat beside him, and Shelton turned his head to meet his bright gaze.

"Enjoying yourself?" Nevil asked. "You look relaxed... and very edible," he continued, making Shelton's blood surge as he looked from Shelton's bare shoulders down his chest, through the water to his blue swimming shorts. He leaned closer and took Shelton's earlobe between his teeth, biting gently, making Shelton shudder with surprise and desire.

Shelton lifted his shoulder. "Nevil!"

"What? Everyone's gone inside," Nevil reminded him, alluding to the young couple and their boisterous children who'd shared the swimming area with them earlier. Shelton darted a quick glance over the pool.

"But anyone could come out... Hell with it," Shelton muttered when Nevil licked the sensitive skin behind his ear. He slid an arm around Nevil's waist and pulled him onto his lap. Nevil straddled him, making happy little humming noises as he rubbed his clothed dick against Shelton's.

"Are you ready for tomorrow?" Nevil asked and licked along Shelton's jawline. Shelton didn't answer, merely seized Nevil's nibbling lips and kissed him thoroughly.

Nevil pulled back, resting his forehead on Shelton's to gaze into his eyes, his own warm and fond. "Hey."

"Hey yourself. And yes, I'm fucking ready to marry you."

Nevil's eyes widened, and then he burst out laughing. A grin tugged Shelton's lips. He rarely cussed, and he enjoyed Nevil's reaction. Delight danced in Nevil's eyes, and he twined his arms around Shelton's neck, pressing their bare chests together under the water. Shelton loved the feel of Nevil's sleek skin against him and groaned into Nevil's mouth when he rocked their hips together and kissed him again.

"We need to get naked," Nevil said raggedly when they came up for air. Shelton grunted, too caught up in the body rutting against him to speak. He trailed his fingers down Nevil's sides, laughing when Nevil jumped at a ticklish spot. Emboldened, giddy with the joy curling inside him, he ran his hands up Nevil's thighs and under his shorts, touching the hard cock with a teasing finger.

Nevil groaned and nipped Shelton's bottom lip, his breath hot and quick against his skin. "God, Shelton, let's go inside," he pleaded, and Shelton's blood surged, knowing he'd brought that quaver to Nevil's voice, the tremble to the hands splayed against his chest.

Hot water bubbled around them, caressing his skin, cradling them in a warm, intimate cocoon. The cool breeze touched his cheeks and Shelton glanced at the stars, thrilling at the beauty of the moment. He felt like he'd been waiting his entire life for Nevil to be his, and by this time tomorrow, Nevil would be wearing his ring. The thought sobered him.

"Am I being selfish?" he asked against Nevil's neck. Nevil leaned away, giving him a questioning look. Shelton took a breath. "You never wanted to marry—"

Nevil's descending mouth stopped his words in a swift kiss. Shelton moved, impatient, needing an answer, but Nevil threaded fingers through his curls, holding him in place while he deepened the kiss, dragging a hungry moan from Shelton's chest. He eased back, cupping Shelton's cheeks in his hands, and ran a thumb over his swollen lips.

"I said I didn't need a piece of paper to prove my commitment," Nevil told him, his expression earnest. "But I've changed my mind. I want you to wear my ring. I want the whole world to know you're mine and I'm yours, for as long as you want me."

"Even forever?" Shelton's voice broke.

Nevil's lips curled in a tender smile. "Always." He stood abruptly, and Shelton scrambled not to slip under the water with the sudden movement. Nevil chuckled and held out a hand. "Come on. I want to try something."

Nevil pulled Shelton to his feet, and he watched Nevil climb the steps from the pool, licking his lips at how Nevil's wet shorts clung to his heavy cock. Shivering in the chill air, he hurried after Nevil into the men's shower room. Nevil stripped as he crossed the tiled floor, hanging his suit on a nearby hook and turning on a shower. Shelton bit his lip, wondering how long it would be before someone else came in to use the pool. Nevil's smirk goaded him into removing his own swimming trunks and joining him under the warm spray.

To his surprise, Nevil soaped up and handed Shelton the bar, rinsing off while Shelton did the same. When done, Nevil turned off the faucet and grabbed Shelton's hand, leading him toward the back of the room. His eyes danced with suppressed excitement. "Come on."

Nevil snatched up towels from a shelf and tossed Shelton one, wrapping his around his slim hips. Warmth flushed through Shelton, and he quickly donned his towel as Nevil opened the door to the sauna room. He hesitated in the doorway while Nevil poured a little water on the glowing coals, making them hiss and steam.

"Someone might—"

Nevil reached over and grabbed the knot on Shelton's towel, tugging him into the room. The door closed with a soft thud, the heat and scent of cedar surrounding them.

"Our wet trunks out there should be warning enough," Nevil said, nibbling Shelton's chin. "If not," he continued, working his lips along Shelton's jaw, "they'd better knock, huh?" He looked up, and Shelton shivered at the fire in his gaze. "Don't worry, love. What I have in mind won't take long."

He nudged Shelton toward the nearest bench, pushing him down gently. After tossing aside his own towel, he leaned over him and untied the knot in Shelton's towel, spreading it open to reveal his rock-hard dick.

"Beautiful," Nevil said and licked his lips. A small pain squeezed Shelton's heart, and he glanced aside, knowing he was scarred and ugly beside Nevil's perfectly molded cock. Nevil's finger touched his chin, turning him back to meet his flashing eyes.

"Fucking gorgeous," he assured Shelton, then dropped to his knees on the wooden flooring and took Shelton into the wet warmth of his mouth. Oh God!

"So good," Shelton groaned, clenching his hands at his sides to keep from thrusting upwards when he nudged into Nevil's throat and Nevil swallowed around him. So good, Nevil driving him mad by slow degrees with teeth and tongue. Nevil tightened his lips, and he sucked Shelton hard as he pulled back off him. The tip of his wicked tongue dipped into the slit at the tip, teeth lightly scraping the ridge, making Shelton shudder with bliss.

Nevil swallowed Shelton again, moving up and down on him, relentless, building his pleasure. Sweat beaded on his forehead, slicked his skin from the heat in the room and the fire Nevil built inside him. Shelton jumped when Nevil gave his thigh a stinging slap, the signal for Shelton to stop being so nice. Absolutely! Shelton gripped Nevil's dark hair with both hands and thrust his hips up, fucking Nevil's generous mouth, watching in awe as his dick slid back and forth between those perfect lips. Could anything be more beautiful?

Nevil hummed around him, and Shelton lost it, his pleasure building with each frantic thrust of his cock. Sweat dripped from his body from the humid air and his frantic need to come. Pressure built to a delicious pitch, his balls pulling up tight to his body.

"Nevil," he warned. Nevil pulled off him, Shelton's dick escaping his lips with a pop. Nevil instantly climbed onto his lap, straddling him as he smashed their lips together. The tang of precome in Nevil's mouth drove Shelton wild, the crush of their balls pushing him toward ecstasy. Nevil gripped both their dicks and pumped them, and Shelton gave in, groaning Nevil's name as fire tore through him, streaming out in spurts of semen between them. Nevil jerked in his arms, and then he came as well, his spunk warm on Shelton's heated chest.

Shelton didn't know how long he floated, warm and sated, but the slam of an outside door jolted him into sitting straight. Nevil chuckled and climbed off him, grabbing up his towel and wiping his chest before wrapping it around his waist. Shelton followed his lead in quick order, praying the door wouldn't open. Nevil's smirk didn't help, though the laughter in his face made him irresistible, and Shelton gave him a kiss before going to the door and easing it open.

Nevil slapped a hand against the door and shoved, walking boldly into the shower room. "No one's here," he called over his shoulder, voice shaking with glee.

"There might have been," Shelton grumbled as he stalked after him, though he admitted to himself he wouldn't trade these stolen moments with Nevil for anything. Nevil insisted on pushing Shelton outside his comfort zone, and Shelton couldn't live without it.

They rinsed under the shower and then pulled on the bathrobes provided for guests, Shelton gathering their swimsuits. Nevil took his hand as they left the pool area and made their way up the back staircases to their room on the top floor. It had grown dark outside, and once inside their room, Shelton pulled the curtains closed on the large picture window with its spectacular view of Mt. Hood, while Nevil knelt and lit the kindling waiting in the stone fireplace.

All the rooms in the lodge were rustic and homey, bright with handmade rugs and quilts. A king-sized bed dominated the center of the room with a small couch before the fireplace, a table and two chairs against the wall. Nevil had thrown a quilt over the television on the dresser, and Shelton heartily agreed, not wanting the world to intrude on this special time.

Going to the small refrigerator under the sink, Nevil took out the complimentary bottle of wine and poured them both a glass, joining Shelton on the couch. He brushed Shelton's fingertips with his own when Shelton reached for his wineglass and clinked the crystal together.

"To the love of my life," he murmured, eyes bright, stealing Shelton's breath. Shelton swayed toward him, not caring that he nearly spilled the pale wine when their lips met in a warm, sweet kiss.

"I love you, Nevil," he said against the mouth he worshipped.

Nevil pressed into the kiss with a soft moan. "I love you too." He settled back on the couch, his expression content and happy. Shelton snuggled against him, head on his shoulder, and watched the fire dancing on the hearth with Nevil's strong heartbeat close to his ear. Finishing his wine, he placed the glass on the floor and stretched out on the couch, laying his head in Nevil's lap as he faced the fire.

"Sleepy?" Nevil asked, playing with Shelton's curls.

"Happy," Shelton countered and slid his hand under Nevil's robe, resting it on his strong thigh. They sat in companionable silence, listening to the crackle of the fire and the occasional sound of a closing door elsewhere in the lodge.

His lids grew heavy, and he'd begun to nod off when Nevil stirred. "Are you getting hungry?"

Shelton chuckled and tightened his hold on Nevil's thigh, loving his sharp breath in response. He rolled to his back and looked up into Nevil's flashing eyes.

"I meant for dinner, sweetheart," Nevil told him and ran a finger down Shelton's chest where the robe had parted. "But if you want something else..."

Shelton's stomach took that moment to rumble loudly, and they both laughed. Shelton gave Nevil what he hoped to be a lurid wink. "Maybe dinner first, then... um... dessert?"

Nevil's gaze smoldered. "Count on it."

Shelton climbed from the couch, holding out a hand to help Nevil to his feet. They lingered over a kiss and then dressed and made their way to the cellar bar, a more intimate area than the formal dining room on the second level of the lodge. Finding a table tucked in the corner, they ordered beer and pizza, chatting in pleasant conversation about anything other than the coming wedding day. Nevil's overt flirting kept Shelton on the edge of arousal, and at one point, Nevil picked up his hand and kissed his knuckles.

"Eat your fill," he warned Shelton, turning his hand and placing a heated kiss in the center of his palm. "I'm not letting you out of our room again tonight."

A delicious shudder traveled Shelton's body, and he finished the slice of pizza he'd been nibbling, anxious to return to their room and the joy of Nevil's arms.

*

Shelton blinked his eyes open and lay a moment listening to Nevil breathing beside him, body warm against his back. Nevil's arm possessively draped his hip and Shelton let out a contented sigh, stretching, deliciously sore in all the right places from last night's lovemaking.

Nevil murmured into Shelton's neck, the hand on his hip reaching down to brush against his cock. He laughed, rolling over to face him. Nevil smiled into his eyes and kissed him, pulling Shelton closer, and he groaned when their cocks slid together perfectly.

"I can never get enough of you," he confessed, rocking against Nevil.

"You're not alone." Nevil nibbled his collarbone, making him shiver. "But we'd better hit the shower if we want to meet the others for breakfast."

"True," Shelton said and slid his hand between them, holding them together. "Wouldn't do to be late... oh..." His thoughts unraveled as Nevil shoved into his hand, the friction of his cock against Shelton's sending off sparks behind his eyes. His pleasure mounted in leaps, and he went with it, letting Nevil lead him to the edge and over, into bliss.

The shower afterwards proved just as pleasurable, though he did nothing but soap Nevil's body, his hands gliding over toned muscles, strong thighs, and a muscular ass. He loved the feel of the fine hair on Nevil's chest under his slick palms, and he took a moment to pinch the tight nubs between his fingers, grinning at Nevil's sharp gasp.

Nevil retaliated by biting Shelton's lower lip and sucking in into his mouth. He grabbed Shelton's wrists when he slid his hands down Nevil's body. "Stop, love! I need to save a little energy for our wedding night."

Shelton laughed, thrilled to the core at Nevil's words. Nevil had set up their wedding plans, reserving several weeks at the lodge, and hired the minister. But these teasing words made it all real for Shelton.

"I love you," he said against Nevil's mouth and kissed him as tenderly and thoroughly as he knew how. They rinsed off, and Shelton handed Nevil a towel when they climbed from the shower. Their room held the warmth from last night's fire, and they dressed leisurely, Nevil stealing kisses every few minutes until Shelton's head swam and he wanted nothing more than to grab Nevil by his chic tie, shove him on the couch, and remove every stitch of clothing he'd just put on.

The thought must have shown on his face. A wicked gleam entered Nevil's turquoise eyes, but he touched Shelton's elbow, guiding him toward the door. "Breakfast?"

"You'll pay for this," Shelton assured him, grinning at Nevil's delighted chuckle as they stepped into the hallway. The main dining room waited a floor below theirs, serving breakfast until eleven, and Shelton's mouth watered as they entered the second level and warmth from the fireplace and the smell of pancakes and coffee enveloped them.

"Shelton! Nevil!" a merry voice called, and Shelton looked across the room to find Tera waving from the dining room entrance. Robert stood beside her, and Shelton smiled to see baby Sarah looking at them from his arms with wide blue eyes under silky dark hair. At six months old, she'd become an adorable little person, and Shelton hurried to take her from her doting father.

"Hi Sarah. Are you ready for an exciting day?" he asked, laughing when she gurgled and smiled at him. She wiggled until he put her up to his shoulder, where she immediately grabbed a handful of his curls. He bit back a painful hiss, and Nevil came to his rescue.

"It's okay, baby girl," Nevil told Sarah as he unwound the chestnut strands from her little fingers. "I can't resist them either."

Nevil cocked his head, his gaze turning speculative as he studied them, and Shelton squirmed under his scrutiny. "What?"

"You look good with a baby in your arms. We may have to do this one day."

For a second, Shelton lost his breath, and a fond smile touched Nevil's lips. He leaned close and kissed the corner of Shelton's mouth. "Not too soon, love," he murmured. "I want to keep you to myself for a while longer. But one day... maybe."

Shelton's heart stumbled, and he blinked at a few tears. "Deal," he managed through a tight throat, wanting to drag Nevil somewhere private and thank him thoroughly. Delight sparkled in Nevil's eyes as he read his mind with ease. Nevil glanced over Shelton's shoulder, and those same gorgeous eyes flashed. A wry grin tugged his lips.

Shelton swiveled his gaze. A young man approached them, ridiculously attractive in a bulky sweater and skinny jeans, red hair hidden to some degree under a black beanie. Mischief danced on his face, and, catching

Shelton's stare, he purposefully moistened full lips made for naughty things...

Nevil's soft chuckle in his ear pulled Shelton's attention back to him. "That boy's trouble," Shelton confessed, heat flushing his neck and cheeks.

"I'll protect you," Nevil promised dryly, stepping forward. "Hey, Tommy..."

Tommy Stephens nodded to him, but came right up to Shelton, his grin widening. "Who's this little cutie?" he asked, smiling at Sarah, who returned his look with solemn eyes.

"This is Nevil's niece. Sarah Marie, this is Tommy. You're never to speak to boys like him."

Tommy laughed and looked into his face, and Shelton caught his breath at the open approval and invitation in his pretty eyes. Heat swept him, and his body stirred, and then Shelton laughed at his own foolishness. Sure, Tommy was attractive: sweet dessert and temptation. Yet easy to put aside in the face of everything he had with Nevil.

As if sensing his answer, Tommy smiled ruefully and handed Shelton the letter he carried. "This just arrived for you."

"Thanks. Are you working today, then?"

"I'm going to ski for a couple hours and then work this afternoon. In fact, I'll be working your reception."

Shelton couldn't think of anything polite to say. "Oh."

Tommy winked. "Maybe I'll get to dance with the groom?" he asked slyly.

"Maybe..." Shelton let his words trail off. Tommy chuckled and walked away, waving over his shoulder.

Nevil looked after him, thinning his lips. "I'll break his legs if he tries to dance with you," he said in a conversational tone.

"Nevil! He's only flirting. You know he can't help it."

"You're defending him?" Robert asked, the reproach unexpected. Shelton shot him a glance and realized he was joking. Tera's fond laugh sent hot blood stinging his cheeks.

"Don't mind us, Shelton," she said, taking Sarah back, pausing while Nevil once again untangled Shelton's curls from her little fingers. "We can't help teasing you. You're adorable when you blush."

Shelton blinked after her while the family moved into the dining room. Nevil's hand warmed the small of his back. "Who's the letter from?"

Shelton looked at the return address, and his heart sank, though the missive hadn't been unexpected. He'd set up his mail to be forwarded just for this reason. "It's from my parents," he said, opening the reply card sent with the wedding invitations. "They won't make it, but hope we'll be happy."

"At least that's something." Nevil slipped his arms around Shelton, pulling him close. "I'm sorry they've let you down."

Shelton shrugged off his disappointment. "It's not the first time, though waiting to send the card at the last minute is a bit much. Anyway, let's eat. I'm starving."

Nevil tightened his hold for a second and then led Shelton into the dining room. Shelton came to a stop halfway across the room, awe sweeping him. "For us?" he asked, wonder in his voice. Sunlight streamed in the windows, highlighting the table reserved in the corner. Candles flickered between attractive bowls of fruit and pastry while fresh coffee waited in china cups at each plate. Gold and silver streamers and tiny bells hung from the ceiling over the table, adding to the delightful scene.

Shelton turned to Nevil, his heart in his eyes. "You did this for me?"

Nevil picked up his left hand, pressing a kiss to his ring finger. "I love you, Shelton, and can't wait to make you my husband. You have my heart, darling."

"Me too," Shelton choked out, wiping at his eyes as he hurried to the chair Tera pulled out for him. Nevil took the seat beside him and proceeded to steal kisses while they ate. By the second cup of coffee, Shelton had regained his composure, though he didn't believe his heart could hold any more joy. He glanced over, idly curious, when a couple entered the dining room, then rose to his feet, a grin spreading on his face. Nevil looked up at him.

"It's Paul and Eran. They made it." Shelton hurried around the table, hand outstretched.

Paul ignored his hand, pulling Shelton into a tight hug. "Congratulations! I couldn't be happier for you. What a great day."

"It is," Shelton agreed, stepping back.

Eran gave him a shy smile and hugged Shelton as well. "Congratulations." He flicked Paul a playful look. "We flew into Portland last night, and Paul insisted on sightseeing..."

Paul threw his hands in the air. "Yes, it's my fault we're getting here so late. But there's a lot to do in Portland on a Friday night, and I lost track of the time. We ended up sleeping in later than I'd planned."

Nevil came up to them. "You didn't miss the wedding. That's the main thing. Thanks again, Paul, for keeping an eye on Shelton in Colorado for me," Nevil said as they shook hands.

"And I made sure to have his favorite drinks ready," Eran put in with a laugh. He worked as the barista at the coffee shop Shelton and Paul had favored after work.

"Thank you so much for coming. I know it means a lot to Shelton," Nevil told them warmly "Are you staying in Portland for a few days?"

"For the week," Eran said. "Paul has a list of places for us to visit."

Nevil nodded. "Excellent. Maybe we can meet for dinner one night."

"Wouldn't want to intrude on the honeymoon." Paul quirked a brow at Shelton, who felt the heat of a blush in his face.

Nevil chuckled at his discomfiture. "Don't worry. We're staying here a couple of weeks, but we're also taking time off this summer to honeymoon right. We're going on one of those cruises to the Mediterranean."

"Sounds fabulous," Eran said. "I'm jealous."

"I'm counting the days." Nevil slid his gaze over Shelton. "I can't wait to see my husband all golden-skinned from the sun."

Shelton swallowed, the warmth in his face travelling lower. Paul's knowing laugh did nothing to help.

"Bastard," he said in an aside to Nevil, who was leering at him, and motioned to the table. "Come and have breakfast. They've given us enough food for an army."

"This is lovely," Eran observed, taking the chair Paul pulled out for him.

"Isn't it? Nevil did this for me. I'm totally being spoiled."

"You deserve it," Tera said from across the table. His friends greeted one another merrily, and Shelton sat back in his chair as they gushed over the baby, his heart swelling once again. Maybe his parents and brother had chosen not to share the day with him, but these were the people who mattered.

Nevil met his gaze and picked up his hand, leaning over to give him a deep kiss while the others were preoccupied.

"Happy?"

"Yes," Shelton said, kissing him back.

*

After breakfast, they parted at the dining room entrance, going to their separate rooms while Paul and Eran took a tour of the lodge. They would dress in Tera's room when it neared time for the wedding. As Shelton's best man, Paul had a tux stashed in the rental car. Eran assured them he'd dress appropriately. Paul's gaze heated as he looked at the dark beauty at his side, and Shelton exchanged a glance with Nevil, wondering if another wedding loomed on the horizon. Nevil grinned and took his elbow, leading him toward the stairs.

"Don't start making plans for our friends, love," Nevil teased as they climbed the steps and followed the hallway to their room. He let them in with his key and then leaned with his back to the closed door, pulling Shelton's unresisting body into his arms.

"I love you," Nevil confessed and kissed him over and over until he lost his breath.

Shelton pushed away from him with a laugh. "We'd better dress. The wedding's at one, and it's already passed noon."

"Afraid they'll start without us?" Nevil stalked him across the room, pressing up against Shelton when he stopped at the closet door. His hard cock pushed against Shelton's ass, and he turned in Nevil's arms, meeting his descending lips.

"God, I love this," Nevil groaned against Shelton's neck, grinding against his hip. "I can't wait to fuck my husband for the first time."

Fire surged through Shelton at his words. "I want that too," he assured Nevil, placing hot kisses along his shaven jawline, nibbling at his lips until they opened. Delicious! Warm and wet and tasting of Nevil. Shelton could kiss him for hours and not get enough of him. Nevil shifted, and a groan burst from Shelton as their cocks ground together. Nevil put a hand behind Shelton's head, holding him in place as he deepened their kiss. Shelton's head reeled, and he forgot everything but Nevil's taste and touch and the scent of his heated skin.

Nevil pulled away from him, and Shelton blinked, momentarily confused. Nevil touched his mouth with an unsteady thumb. "You are such a temptation, love," he said, his voice ragged. "We'd better dress before I can't stop myself and make us very late for the wedding."

It took a moment for Nevil's words to penetrate the haze of lust Shelton had fallen into. "Oh. Okay," he murmured, making Nevil chuckle. He grinned sheepishly, adjusting his cramped dick. "Promise me we'll pick up where we left off?"

Nevil's gaze had followed Shelton's hand. "Count on it," he said, sounding strangled. Joy bubbled up in Shelton and he laughed to ease the tightness in his chest.

It took only moments for them to strip out of their clothes, and they dressed in their respective tuxedoes, Nevil devastating in black with a charcoal shirt. Shelton wore pristine white with a charcoal tie that brought out the green in his hazel eyes. Nervous, he had trouble with the tie and met Nevil's gaze in the mirror when he came up behind him. Shelton caught his breath, heart leaping at the love and naked desire in Nevil's expression. Nevil turned him, and Shelton felt the tremble in his fingers as he knotted his tie.

"Hey you," he whispered. Nevil looked up, and Shelton's heart lurched at the gleam of tears in his eyes. He tenderly cupped Nevil's face. "Is this what you want, honey? We can still call it off and just have a party."

"Absolutely not. With how gorgeous you look right now, no way are we stepping outside this lodge without my ring on your finger."

Shelton snorted, though warmth spread through him at Nevil's words. They left the room, and Nevil's hand on the small of his back as they took the hallway and stairs to the second floor helped steady Shelton's nerves. They passed other guests staying at the lodge, many who offered them congratulations. Shelton hardly noticed them as they crossed the second floor, skirted the central fireplace, and took the small hallway in the back.

His heart hammered with nerves and anticipation as they climbed the stairs to the Eagle's Nest at the top of the lodge. Sunlight spilled through the open doorway, and Shelton paused on the threshold, losing his breath in wonderment. Sunlight flooded the space through the floor-to-ceiling windows looking out over the mountains at either end of the room, the bright rays gleaming off the oak floors and walls. White linen and silver candles and flowers adorned the tables in the back of the hall, while chairs in front held their friends. An archway of gardenia and pink cabbage roses stood in the far window where the minister waited with Tera and Paul.

Catching sight of them, the violinist switched to the song they'd chosen, and Nevil tugged Shelton's hand, leading him to the back of the room. Their friends stood, turning to them, and Shelton wondered if his pounding heart would burst out of his chest.

Nevil's hand found his, warm and sure. "Ready, love?"

Shelton looked at him and saw his own love reflected in Nevil's warm gaze. "Yes," he said, gripping Nevil's hand as they walked toward their friends and the start of their new life together.

About Dianne Hartsock

Dianne is the author of m/m romance, paranormal suspense, fantasy adventure, the occasional thriller, and anything else that comes to mind. She lives in the beautiful Willamette Valley of Oregon with her incredibly patient husband, who puts up with the endless hours she spends hunched over the keyboard letting her characters play. She says Oregon's raindrops are the perfect setting in which to write. There's something about being cooped up in the house with a fire crackling on the hearth and a cup of hot coffee warming her hands that kindles her imagination.

Currently, Dianne works as a floral designer in a locally-owned gift shop, which is the perfect job for her. When not writing, she can express herself through the rich colors and textures of flowers and foliage.

Facebook
www.facebook.com/diannehartsock

Twitter
@diannehartsock

Website
www.diannehartsock.wordpress.com

Other NineStar books by this author

Callum's Fate

Sweet William

The Mirror Maze

Little Match Girl

Luka

Birthday Presents

Also from NineStar Press

Birthday Presents by Dianne Hartsock

Crimson loves to dance. He adores watching the pretty boys grind to the frantic beat of the music and picking out his lover for the evening. But more than that, he lives for his birthday, that one day a year he gives into his darker impulses: choosing a young man to lure into the alleyway with promises of sex, then slitting his throat in the midst of their passion and reveling in the hot blood on his hands.

For Tracey Winston, life has become a nightmare. Kidnapped from a nightclub in Boulder, Colorado, brutalized and raped by Crimson, he's held captive in a cabin in the Rocky Mountains along with sweet Kyle, a young man Crimson keeps chained to his bed and is slowly torturing to death. Though Tracey manages to escape with Kyle's help, he has to leave Kyle behind in Crimson's cruel hands.

Detective Gene Mallory has never stopped looking for his brother Kyle, kidnapped from a nightclub seven months previously. The case breaks open when Tracey Winston comes forth at the urging of his new boyfriend, claiming to have knowledge of where Crimson is hiding out. A manhunt begins with Crimson continuously slipping through their net. Lives are on the line, with both Gene and Tracey being targeted by the killer. A traitor in their midst tips Crimson off to their plans.

Crimson's birthday has come and gone, and he will kill again.

Luka by Dianne Hartsock

Luka makes a desperate wish and the earth shifts to his will. Regretting it immediately, he tries to undo the sorcery, but it is too late. He asked for hope, and to his horror, all the hope in the world is given into his keeping. He desires nothing more than to return this gift to the world.

Aethan wants to get his hands on the Well of Hope in Luka's keeping. If he can ransom out hope to others at his whim, the world will be at his feet. Where it belongs.

With the aid of his lover, Rhys, Luka stays one step ahead of Aethan. But Rhys has his own enemy in Aethan, his estranged father.

Rescued by Luka, his sweet, gentle witch, Rhys now stands with him against Aethan. They have vowed to return the Well of Hope to the earth despite all odds, or die trying. For what is life worth, for anyone, without hope?

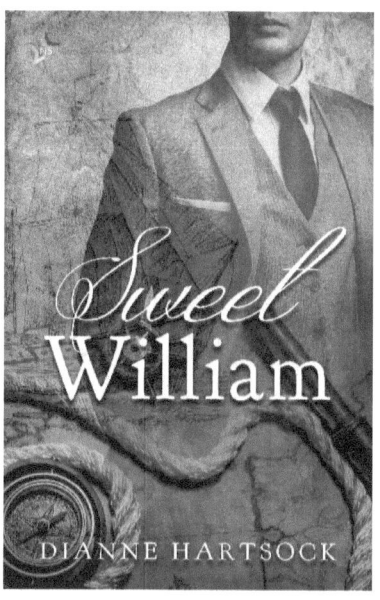

Sweet William by Dianne Hartsock

William Wilkerson leads the life of the privileged rich. Head of his father's shipping business, he indulges to his heart's content in the pleasures of the flesh with Boston's finest young men.

That is, until he reunites with Fredrick: his former tutor and the one man who captured his heart. But William's father has declared Fredrick off limits. And Fredrick, himself, believes he's beneath the attention of the Wilkerson heir.

After having lost his current pupil to graduation, and with no prospects of a replacement, Frederick is homeless, hungry, and easy pickings for the men on the docks. When

Frederick is shanghaied into service on William's own merchant ship, will William discover his plight in time to rescue him?

Connect with NineStar Press

www.ninestarpress.com

www.facebook.com/ninestarpress

www.facebook.com/groups/NineStarNiche

www.twitter.com/ninestarpress

www.instagram.com/ninestarpress

www.ingramcontent.com/pod-product-compliance
Lightning Source LLC
Chambersburg PA
CBHW050401260626
47156CB00003B/819